MW01627626

THE FIFTH GENERATION
A Nez Perce Tale

THE FIFTH GENERATION
A Nez Perce Tale

Linwood Laughy

This is a work of fiction. Names, characters, places and incidents are the product of the author's imagination or are used fictitiously. Any resemblance to actual persons, living or dead, business establishments, events or locales is entirely coincidental.

Published by Mountain Meadow Press
Box 447
Kooskia, Idaho 83539-0447

Publisher's Cataloging in Publication

Laughy, Linwood.

The fifth generation : a Nez Perce tale / Linwood Laughy.

p. cm.
ISBN-13: 978-0-945519-24-9
ISBN-10: 0-945519-24-9

1. Nez Perce Indians--Fiction. 2. Nez Perce Indians--History--Fiction. 3. Indians of North America--Northwest, Pacific--Fiction. 4. Lewis and Clark Expedition--(1804-1806)--Fiction. 5. Idaho--History--Fiction. 6. Historical fiction, American. I. Title.

PS3612.A9435F54 2010 813'.6
QBI09-600128

Printed in the United States of America

Book cover painting *Bear Shaman III* by Carol Hagan of Carol Hagan Studios, Billings, Montana.

Acknowledgments

Excerpts from *Choup-nit-ki, With the Nez Perce,* by E. Jane Gay, published with permission from the Schlesinger Library, Radcliffe Institute for Advanced Study, Harvard University.

Excerpts from *In Pursuit of the Nez Perces,* Part I by Oliver Otis Howard, published with permission from Mountain Meadow Press.

The past is never dead. It is not even the past.

William Faulkner

It is but justice to say that the whole nation to which these people belong are the most friendly, honest, and ingenious people we have seen in the course of our voyage and travels.

Sergeant Patrick Gass
Lewis & Clark Expedition
July 4, 1806

During the late 18th century, according to tribal oral history, Nez Perce spiritual leaders predicted that a major change was coming to their culture. This change would come from the east, the *tewats* said, and the Nez Perce people would have difficult times for five generations.

PROLOGUE

1953

Isaac hoisted his pack and stepped off his porch exactly at midnight. He carried a crowbar like an abbreviated cane, its curved end filling the inside of his fist, chiseled tip dangling above the ground. He walked briskly down the trail that led from his two-room house in a wooded draw to the narrow road that paralleled the river west. Broken clouds swept up the valley, smearing dark patches on the moonlit landscape. Gravel crunched underfoot. A screech owl called for a mate.

A mile downstream, the middle span of a railroad bridge balanced on a stone-filled crib bucking the spring current. A red fir floater lodged momentarily against the bridge's center pier, snapped its top and continued its journey. He stepped from tie to tie between the polished rails in familiar sequence.

On the south side of the river, a sweat lodge squatted on a cobble beach edged by dogbane and willow.

Crowbar propped against a cedar drift log, he removed the cold stones from the lodge's center to the fire pit outside and tucked the battered milk pail used for dipping water beneath a clump of cottonwood roots overhanging the riverbank. He wanted the sweat lodge ready, he told himself, though he had no idea when he might return. His plan began at midnight, ended at 3:00 a.m., and was as empty beyond as most of the past ten years of his life. He was running on faith, on the blood in his veins, on the voices and the dreams.

With crowbar back in hand, he strode east on the railroad track two ties at a time, even when a thick cloud blurred the edges of the creosoted ties. At half a mile he pushed upslope through hackberry and hawthorn, then paused beneath a massive bull pine at the edge of a patch of grass where marble and granite headstones kept vigil in the night. With a flashlight he checked his watch, then slowed his pace to the third row south and gave a military headstone a respectful nod.

Swinging the crowbar in a brief arc beside his swollen right knee, he crossed No Kid Lane and waded through alfalfa ready for the season's first cutting. Across the field, streetlights glowed through soft patches of mist. At Hill and First, a dog barked. A scrawny cat followed him a short way, then disappeared as another cloud darkened the valley.

He skirted a streetlight and entered the alley just west of Main. A sharp corner of the envelope under his shirt pricked his chest as he followed the alley south. In the car lot behind the Texaco station he leaned the crowbar against the chromed bumper of a '47 coupe, cautious now as he approached the center of the five-block town. Three stores north, the metal lid of the post office box squeaked as he lowered it into place after dropping the envelope into the opened slot. The rest of Main lay quiet as unsuspecting prey. For a moment he remembered cheering crowds lining both sides of the street, the high school pep band playing on a tractor-drawn trailer, state championship trophy in his hands. He was glad now for the silence, shadows lying flat on the pavement, pickups with their toolboxes and slip tanks still parked beside the curb.

The swinging crowbar matched his gate east on 5th. Beneath a street lamp his watch read 12:48, and a half block later he again turned north. At the far end of the alley, he set his pack on the lid of a galvanized garbage can and felt for his folding meat saw. Its metal blade scraped the side of his flashlight as the saw slid into his left pants pocket. Leather gloves were next, twisted together and stuffed under his belt. Pack stowed on top of the cardboard and bottles that filled the garbage can two-thirds full, he tucked his hair beneath the collar of his Levi jacket and pulled his cap bill low on his face.

The chisel end of the crowbar snagged momentarily at the hole he'd cut earlier in the evening in the bottom of his right pants pocket, then glided along his thigh to below his knee with an unexpected chill. With the crowbar's crook lipped over the pocket's edge, he took a step, then two, adjusting his stride to a familiar limp. The click of hard steel against the copper rivet at the corner of the pocket joined the heightened sound of his breathing as he crossed Fourth.

It was exactly 1:00 a.m. when Isaac Moses stepped over the curb and opened the side door to the Boots & Saddles Bar.

CHAPTER ONE

1918

Jimmy Girardoux and Henry Old Beaver caught their breaths as they crested a bony ridge on the south side of the valley, then settled onto a patch of bunchgrass with spring sun on their backs. Far below, two sets of buildings clustered on opposite sides of the river that carved the canyon north, then bent due west toward the sea. The smaller group was Indian Village—a white-washed church, a missionary house flat gray beside a brief ravine, a clapboard school and teacherage, a few slab houses settled amongst the pines. A mile down-stream stood the town of Kamiah, with streets and houses surrounding Main like the lines and squares on a game board. Nearby, the tipi burner from a sawmill etched a plume of smoke onto the scene. A wagon bridge spanned the river north of town, and railroad tracks crossed a narrows farther west. Beyond the river a log flume snaked down a south-facing slope, a ribbon of wood and water and perpetual progress, the constant goal of Kamiah's merchants.

"It's a white man's war!" Henry's declaration was as firm as the layers of basalt that lay beneath them. "If some Indian boys have to go over there, let them Carlisle Christians go. They're the ones always backing up the white man."

Jimmy sat silently, elbows on knees, thumbs pressed against the bottom of his jaw. A pair of geese glided down the valley, circled, made a slow-motion descent and disappeared into a hidden slough. Henry's words floated with the thermals erasing the last traces of dew from the valley floor—first fog, then mist, now barely discernable wisps.

"The war isn't even in this country," Henry continued. Anger edged his words now, sharpened by the fear of losing his friend as well as his argument, of bearing witness to the possible ending in his life of something precious and irreplaceable. He tried to read his friend's stance, the slope of his shoulders, the angle of his cradled jaw.

"Look at that town down there. Is that what you want to die for? Remember that sign on the White Bird bar—*No Dogs or Indians*?"

Jimmy's face turned upstream. His eyes swept the curves of the river like an osprey searching for rainbows in a riffle. He needed a sign to pull him off his finely flaked edge of uncertainty. The only thing he knew for sure was that an enemy could never kill him.

In his thirteenth summer Jimmy for the first time had sat beside death, had talked to his boyhood friend buried near a mountain meadow of gentian beside *Ishana Ishkit*, the trail to the buffalo. The great grandson of a Nez Perce chief, the friend had died of an unknown cause while berry picking with his grandparents. Jimmy's graveside visit was vivid in his memory — the light blue sky, dark blue gentian, purple stains of huckleberry juice on green leaves that would soon paint the hillsides crimson. A circle of white granite outlined the mounded earth, achromatic amidst the hues that surrounded it. Jimmy had gone alone; his family camped a mile away, his parents understanding his wish to make the last leg of this journey by himself. The spirit of the mountain surrounded him then, and he knew he would return when the time arrived to learn his name, to hear his song, to find the guidance that would govern the rest of his life.

He went back the following year, walked from saddle to summit and summit to saddle on this ancient trail, following the path of millennia of youth before him. The venison jerky he carried was gone by noon of his second day of walking, the last piece slowly shredded and absorbed rather than chewed and swallowed, and he began to fast. He left the main trail and climbed a final mile of timbered slope to the top of a worn peak where a rock the size of a pit house sat solidly in the center of a patch of bunchgrass as if dropped from the sky by an errant god.

With stars at arm's length, Jimmy slept. By morning his hunger had vanished. By midday, when his waning thirst had nearly disappeared as well, his dead friend spoke to him in an unmistakable voice: “Gather five huckleberries. Eat them slowly.” Jimmy did as instructed, gently pressing the juice of each berry between his coated tongue and the dry roof of his mouth.

By late afternoon, dark clouds rolled up the ridges from the Lochsa River and covered him in shadow. A chilling breeze became a wind, and Jimmy huddled on the lee side of the rock waiting, his blanket wrapped tightly around him. Finally, his eyes closed and he slid into a trance-like sleep.

In the depth of the night a flash of ice-blue light came hurtling toward him, a piercing promise of death. Suddenly the bolt became an arrow, then slowed and landed in Jimmy's outstretched hand. A second streak came from his left, again became shaft and stone and feather and fell gently at his feet. As he bent to retrieve this arrow, a third flew over him and landed on the stone at his back. Two more times his eyes burned with the intensity of the light that cleaved the blackness around him, and two more times the arrows missed their mark. He had gathered four of the arrows in his dream when a heavy rain lashed his upturned face, flowed along the left side of his nose and into a corner of his mouth.

Four years had passed since this visit to the mountain without the chance to share his new name, his song, his dance—the guardian spirit ritual now a footnote in some anthropologist's report.

“Let’s go.” Henry’s urgent voice broke Jimmy’s spell.

“They raised a lot of money at the war auction yesterday.” Jimmy’s words were directed toward himself as much as toward his friend, “Pipes, quirts, eagle fans. I heard it was more money than they got in town.”

“And it’s their war we’re supporting,” Henry retorted, “selling off our warrior’s weapons like worn out cattle.”

Jimmy could once more hear the lilting voice of the auctioneer, see the nodding heads of buyers at the corners of the gathering of white shirts and calico skirts, buckskin now rare as buffalo. Buyers had come from as far away as Lewiston, serious collectors and dealers mostly, with a dash of Kamiah’s curious. Someone had hoisted an American flag on a makeshift pole in front of the canvas fly that served as a staging area. Two khaki-clad army recruiters glanced at each item at the beginning of a bidding, then surveyed the men in the audience, visually assessing each one’s age, his height and weight, the expression on a face as the gavel fell on the sale of a drum or flute, now objects of the devil sold to save souls and soldiers alike. A warrior’s eagle- bone whistle on a buckskin thong stopped Jimmy’s quiet conversation. “In our war,” was all he said as he watched the bidding intensify, then stall, then march ahead to the “Sold to number 16!” call of the auctioneer. Number 16, the local pawnbroker Bill Sheffield, shared a thin-lipped smile with the gray-haired auction clerk.

The crowd grew quiet when the auctioneer’s assistant placed the last three items on the table —a war shirt decorated with porcupine quills, a yew wood bow in a buckskin case, and the single item of greatest fascination for Jimmy Girardoux, a pipe tomahawk with a lone blue bead embedded in its handle.

The bow went first amidst numbers and nods while Number 16 walked to where Billy Moses stood beside a wagon wheel propped against the pitchy side of a five-inch pine. The two men talked. The white man pointed toward one of the army recruiters, to the table beneath the tent fly, to the missionary house in the background. Billy nodded and looked aside as their right hands clasped, then rose and fell a single time. While the auctioneer caught his breath, Billy stepped to the auction table, retrieved the pipe tomahawk from where he had placed it earlier in the day, then walked to his gelding bay tethered near a spread of wild carrot. Bidder number 9 bought the war shirt with little competition.

Henry stood, seeking a new angle on his argument. "And don't forget who killed your grandfather," he challenged. "That's where our people crossed the river, there where those geese set down. The soldiers were right here on this ridge, and they'd have killed us both if we'd been here then."

Warriors, soldiers, fighting—Henry's words were like three flat rocks in a stream, a bridge over the gap of indecision that had haunted Jimmy for weeks. Step by step, he was crossing to the other side. He stood and sucked the warm spring air deep into his chest. "Let's go," he said softly to his friend.

Henry knew. He understood the quiet eyes, the square of his friend's shoulders, the easy stride as

Jimmy started down the trail in front of him.

"You'll come back dead, that's what will happen." Henry spit out angrily.

"I can never be killed by an enemy," Jimmy responded.

"And what would your grandfather say?" Henry asked, spilling his final argument on the hillside now passing quickly beneath them.

"He would understand. He was a warrior too."

CHAPTER TWO

1952

The powdered dust of ancient bones coated the sticky beads of puke stinging the inside of Isaac's nostrils. The concrete curb jammed against his nose proved insufficient force to stop the rhythmic flow of earth in, blood out. Tobacco juice fresh from the mouth of a stranger oozed along a crease in his neck and dripped onto the street. Somewhere in the night a cat yowled her availability, and when she stopped momentarily, Isaac thought he heard horses galloping across the flat that separated Kamiah's few blocks from the Clearwater River. "The ponies are coming," he muttered to himself. But the hoof beats were in his head, and the steady beat of drums that followed came from his throbbing right shoulder bent into the gutter eight feet from the side door of the Boots & Saddles Bar.

He sat up on the curb and cautiously swung his head from side to side. Straight black hair brushed his shoulders, a length neither white man short nor Indian long; the length, he had once told a friend, of perpetual mourning. He could feel his left eye swelling shut. With the other he scanned Fourth Street—the mottled brick of a former hotel, false wooden storefronts jutting into the night sky. Straight ahead, Main Street stretched south under occasional street lamps— Kamiah Hardware, Johnston's Mercantile, Nickel's Clothing, Jarty's Jewelry, Kamiah Drug, the post office, Texaco station, the Odd Fellows Hall. He had once been welcomed in all of them, had paraded down Main while a Sousa march from the high school band proclaimed the glory of the 1937 Kamiah Kubs' basketball team and their star center, Isaac Moses. His gaze broadened to the rooftops and chimneys of the houses clustered neatly around the business section of town, and in the faint light of a quarter moon, the backdrop of ridges that climbed to prairie plateaus beyond.

The first attempt at a town, a few hundred yards to the north, had nipped at the heels of the opening of the Nez Perce Reservation to white settlement in 1895. The five-year lease of the land on which the town was originally built had justified the ramshackle pile of logs and rough-sawn lumber that emerged beside the riverbank. When merchants purchased an Indian allotment four years later, the town dragged itself to higher ground and hewed its way into a new century. According to local leaders, Kamiah was a friendly, family town. Across the river and upstream a mile, East Kamiah was for Indians.

Main Street now lay ethered in anticipation of the last call for drinks in the two establishments presently open for business. Isaac knew he must be gone by the time the bars closed. If he could make it to the river, he'd find safety in the willows. He'd slept amongst them many nights, too drunk to match his steps to the creosoted ties of the railroad bridge. The first span was forty-five ties long, then ninety-one more to the center. The bridge's north half was six ties shorter, denying symmetrical certitude. In moonlight the ties were visible, as was the rushing water below. On dark nights he counted, using his fingers like rosary beads. The highway bridge a mile upstream was too well lighted for a drunk Indian.

He pushed one knee to the street, winced as a sharp rock dug into his kneecap, then stood. With a final glance up Main, he cornered the bar unsteadily and headed north. Five cracks in the sidewalk brought him to Uncle Bill's Pawn Shop, where he stopped, puked on his well-scuffed Redwing boots, then searched the contents of the pawn shop's display window with the aid of a flickering street light. A fiddle, two vases, radios, a saddle, pocket watches—and blue beads wrapped around the handle of an eagle feather fan. Through this window he had watched his people disappear piece-by-piece—beaded leggings and painted parfleches, cedar root baskets and corn husk bags. At times he had made his own contributions to this slow parade into oblivion. He pressed his face to the window and tried unsuccessfully to retch.

The north end of Main ended abruptly at a straight stretch of U.S. 12. A hayfield beckoned from the other side. The highway quiet, he started across. His journey was familiar—two roads to cross, two barbed wire fences, a patch of brush, and a short distance of railroad track.

A barb ripped his pant leg and raked across the inside of his thigh as he stepped over the top strand of barbed wire at the first fenceline. He lumbered through thick brome and timothy two weeks short of being mowed, baled, bucked and stacked in some white rancher's barn. Near the northwest corner of the field the top strand of wire drooped, and both he and deer made regular use of the fence's disrepair. From there a game trail threaded a patch of thorn bush that curved around the shoulder of a one-acre flat. Raising both arms in front of his face, he pushed through the branches hanging over the trail, one limb eluding his forearms and tracing a thin line of blood along his left cheekbone. He avoided the easier route over open ground where familiar names were etched on slabs of granite scattered amongst the pines—Yellow Bear, Looking Glass, Red Wolf, Black Eagle. His father's name was there as well, *James Girardoux, May 14,1898 -December 10, 1918* on the stained military marble identifying a man Isaac had never known. With two yaps and a high-pitched howl, a coyote across the river announced its loneliness to the night.

The trail led to twin steel rails that paralleled the riverbank. The rails were spiked to treated ties two feet apart in a gravel bed, a crosshatched pattern embroidered across America. He took the first short step, the second. A few ties later voices spilled over the shoulder of the field to his left—Nez Perce, English, French—then shouts and laughter and the labored breathing of men running across the flat. "Drouillard! Drouillard! He wins!" Soon horse hooves beat a rhythm Isaac could feel through the thick ties on which he stood. He smiled. He had heard the ponies after all. More shouts faded into the sound of rushing water a hundred yards away.

Isaac tried two ties to the step, stumbled, started again toward the river with the abbreviated stride the ties demanded. The smell of the river beckoned, and he sidestepped down the graded slope of the railroad bed. Beneath the exposed roots of a cottonwood he found his Levi jacket, flannel lining ripped out of one side, and the battered stadium cushion he kept there for a pillow, *Vandals* printed across its vinyl cover in cracked gold letters. Jacket on, he nestled into a pocket of sand kept dry by the overhang of the riverbank. The sound of the river splashing on quartz and granite sang him to sleep.

A thin mist was lifting off the water by the time Isaac stirred. His legs were stiff and his shoulder ached. His left eye refused to open. He shivered uncontrollably, then crawled to where sunlight bathed the cobble-strewn beach and raised himself to the trunk of a four-foot cedar washed in by last spring's flood. The curve of a root curling up from the base of the trunk provided a backrest. Soon his shaking stopped and a warm glow spread over his face, yellows and reds moving across the insides of his eyelids like summer sunsets. He tried to let the river's song carry away the lingering flotsam of his Saturday night—the beer, the taunts, the shoves, a fist, the doorframe, spit. Wrapped now in warmth, he dozed.

When Isaac awoke, his right eye was focused on the railroad bridge, three separate spans each supported by a rock-filled timber crib pointing upstream like a wayward icebreaker run aground. At the center of the bridge, a circle of cold-rolled steel two inches thick rested on a series of rollers that had once enabled the center span to pivot. Local merchants a half-century earlier had insisted on this expensive feature, confident that sternwheelers would one day conquer the Clearwater's rapids and connect Kamiah to the network of water transportation down the Snake and Columbia to the Pacific. The span had been opened once to demonstrate the bridge's capability, but this proved insufficient invitation to the ships that ceased their struggles against the current at Lewiston 65 miles downstream.

A few times a week an engine crossed the bridge pulling cars filled with lumber from local mills. The railroad's mainstay had once been Camas Prairie grain delivered to the valley floor on cabled tramways, suspended buckets of grain plunging down steep ridges from the prairie's edge. Every fifth bucket would haul supplies uphill to be loaded onto wagons and pulled by horses to the farmhouses strewn across the broken sod. The camas for which the prairie had been named—whose bulb was a staple of the Nez Perce diet—had long been grazed out or plowed under.

Isaac wrapped the stadium cushion in his tattered coat and cached them both in their usual place. Confident that no train would be crossing the bridge on a Sunday morning, he marked his passage with railroad ties, counting each one as if to reassure himself of his world's predictability. At the center of the bridge he sat on the edge of the circle of steel and watched driftwood shoot between the bridge piers, unable to cross to either side of his fractured life.

Minutes passed until Isaac pulled himself upright and started a fresh count of the 91 ties to the last span, and 39 more to shore. At the north end of the bridge he left the tracks and turned upstream on a gravel dike that defined the north edge of the riverbank.

The smell of fresh sawdust rolled up the north side of the dike, the musty odor of willow shoots and wet sand on the south. Four years earlier he had worked at the sawmill that covered most of the flat inside this elbow of the river, had pulled rough lumber off the green chain through a wet spring and dusty summer. He hated the constant noise of the chains and belts and pulleys and sprockets, the odor of gas, grease and oil. "Do this, Chief," his boss would say. By fall he knew he would quit. His family's grocery bill had been paid, he'd retrieved his rifle from the pawnshop, and his first pickup pushed back the blackberry patch at the edge of their makeshift yard.

Narrow bands of sunlight sliced through the canopy of the cottonwoods lining the river's bank as Isaac continued upstream. Two whitetail does skittered away before him, their bellies full with fawn. A merganser led her babies into fast water at his approach. In twenty minutes he came to the trail that led up a narrow draw to his house with yellowed plastic stapled across a broken window, a single shard of glass beneath the plastic pointing nowhere in particular. The hood was raised on his pickup parked near the front porch. A thumb-thick blackberry vine curled over a fender and disappeared beneath the air cleaner. Isaac lived here alone except for the occasional deer that still remembered June pea pods or September squash. Four years earlier his sister Sarah had finished high school, and when a summer romance failed, had left for Seattle. His mother, Mary, had remained two more years watching her parents' house continue to lose its battle with alder and willow and serviceberry. In the summer of '51 she met a Cayuse man at a pow-wow and by first snow had moved to Oregon. Isaac stayed, for the fish and the fruit and the worn familiarity of the trails he followed through the darkness of his life. But mostly he stayed for the voices, waiting for them to tell him who he was and what his life would be.

CHAPTER THREE

1918

Mary Moses left the valley to go forward. Jimmy Girardoux left it to go back. For three brief days their journeys merged as their lives hung suspended in summer heat and cottonwood shade near the river at the bend below the timbered toll bridge. She was fresh from Carlisle Indian School, a *returned one* now, typed and tainted, a new form of breed trained white but wrapped in the same brown skin with which she had left. He was fresh from boot camp, a newfound sureness in his walk, a gaze that did not bend from strangers. His straight black hair was crew-cut short, muscles tight, uniform thrown on the willows at the edge of the sand along this quiet stretch of river, the current's calm unlike their own rushing pace. Later they would take their time, sparks from driftwood dancing on an upstream breeze, loneliness lost in the rhythm wedged between them.

Mary did not dance. The drumming in her soul had been lost along the tracks of the Union Pacific, in the sand hills of Nebraska, in the cemetery behind Hatfield Hall where Carlisle's youthful dead were buried in the Pennsylvania night—brown skin and black hair with names like Rachel, Sarah, Jonah and James. No sound of drums, no sweetgrass smoke, a hurried prayer to a god who spoke neither Nez Perce nor Sioux, Hidatsa nor Crow.

A part of her had also died, a quiet withering within the ordered Carlisle routine. The wilder ones had died in chunks, buckskins burned and black braids swept away in piles. Names were next. "Pick one," the thin-lipped stranger at the front of the classroom had said, pointing to a list of Christian names chalked on sheets of slate that filled the wall before them. "Pick one now." The Navajo boy in the first desk in the left hand row had never heard of a *pikwunnow*. He looked at the marks where the white finger pointed, felt the urgency in that voice, the seriousness in the smile that loomed before him. His cautious grin ended their exchange. "James Smallboy" announced the teacher to a clerk, who wrote the name on a chart behind the teacher's desk. Moving efficiently to the head of the next row of desks, where a Cheyenne girl peered from beneath freshly cut bangs, the white woman once again pointed toward the chalkboard and repeated, "Pick one. Pick one now," sweeping centuries of naming ceremonies across the polished oak floors like troublesome dust.

Mary had been allowed to keep her name, if not her hair, her clothes, her smile. Her preparation for Carlisle had begun on her father's knee, had groomed her as she sat on the edge of the platform at the front of East Kamiah's First Presbyterian Church where her father had taken her every other childhood Sunday, where she had folded her hands and watched brown faces sing praises to the white man Jesus whose image was nailed to the cloth-covered wall—power and grace, mercy and wrath, and forgiveness of the sins that flew out of the big black book like hungry ravens.

Her childhood had been a compromise negotiated between her parents Sunday-by-Sunday and season-by-season. On alternate weeks she followed her mother, Walking Woman, to meadows of camas, hillsides of cous, streams of eels coming home to mate. They picked blackberries on the riverbank, chokecherries in shaded draws, huckleberries on mountain slopes. They sang to the seven roots of their spring feast, to the first salmon that gifted them its rich flesh, to the smooth stones lying quietly in deep pools. Her mother showed her other stones as well—lodge rings hidden in cedar shade and smaller circles of stones on nearby hilltops pinning ancient bones to the ground. Mary learned to speak with her eyes, to ask the many questions of a child in silence, to watch her mother's hands in reply.

Twice a year they followed a narrow stream green with cress, the trail faded on the mottled fabric of the hillside. When the river below them seemed the mere width of a wrist, they would angle into a box canyon, a pocket of shadow surrounded by thick columns of black basalt rising six-sided to the sky. From the back of this roofless cave, an 8-inch stream leapt from the edge of a shelf of rock and offered itself to a pool twenty feet below. Echoes of its landing whispered to Mary and her mother as they waited for sunlight to strike a slab of stone on the right side of the waterfall, a giant canvas stretched taut 6 million years ago, painted figures emerging from the stone in the solstice sun. Yellow buffalo and mountain sheep stood in rows, waiting for red-painted hunters peering out from lichen that framed the scene in grays and greens. Higher on the wall, a series of rays arced above the faces of three figures holding magic wands, spirits looking calmly at Mary and her mother rooted to this ground, these rocks, this water sliding over the lip of the pool and gliding past them. It was here that Mary understood the depth of her mother's ties to their common past, her mother's quiet steps on the sacred ground she found everywhere she walked.

For weeks before Mary's departure for Carlisle she had been pushed and pulled, prayed over and prayed about, her own conflicts mirrored by the silence growing daily between her parents. Her mother's eyes had lost their softness, her father's voice quavered when he spoke. Flight was the final choice for Mary, Carlisle a place to go. Dressed in white shirt and sorrow, her father had taken her to the train depot, horse and wagon moving as if in a funeral procession. Her mother had disappeared the day before with clothes packed, tools bundled, the garden gate ajar. A blue-beaded medicine bag lay on top of Mary's cracked cardboard suitcase—her mother's only goodbye. The size of a sparrow, the bag hung around Mary's neck as the train crossed the river west of town.

By the end of the second day of traveling east, time and distance had settled on Mary like fog, had curled her into a corner at the back of a rail car where she was swallowed by the sights and sounds surrounding her. Peaks and prairies averaged out into one huge span of vastness. Towns and cities melted past, with stops in daylight and dark for farmers, cowboys, priests, lovers, women with babies and baskets. Occasionally, at some lonesome stop with a few families gathered on a wooden platform baking in the dusty day, other Indian children took their first steps into this house on wheels, walked down the narrow aisle, then disappeared behind a tall-backed seat and settled into their own attempts to mark the landscape disappearing from their lives. The rest of Mary's trip was days and nights of fitful sleep across the ends of a million rails separated by clackety gaps.

Smiles. That's what Mary remembered most from when her third or fourth train finally stopped on a tree-lined street in a town of painted houses and flower boxes. Teachers and townsfolk welcomed the frightened faces peering at them, new additions to the cause and the town's economy. Perhaps remembering their own initial arrivals, uniformed students also smiled as they helped with luggage, then rode beside the newcomers on the trolley over the stone bridge at the edge of town and through Carlisle's entrance gate as the dazed recruits reported for their reconstruction, their rehabilitation, their rebirth. After 39 years of practice, Carlisle's mission was carried out with the efficiency of its founding father, Colonel Richard Henry Pratt, whose guiding principle had been chiseled into the minds of teachers and students alike—*Kill the Indian, Save the Man.*

Mary passed through that entrance gate her father's daughter. Pages of prayers and familiar hymns greeted her at chapel every day. English words welcomed her in crowded classrooms. Unlike many of the students who marched each day from dorm to class and gym to church, her government shoes did not disconnect her from the earth. She hid her medicine bag before it was discovered and replaced it around her neck with a metal cross offered as a gift for her compliance. And yet, never stripped of an ancient name, never struck for speaking Nez Perce, never beaten for climbing the wall and escaping into the night, Mary remained one step apart from even her most well-intentioned masters. The wild ones among the students ran, were caught, stockaded, beaten, and finally, as captives often do, learned to love their captors.

Nine months into her transformation, with routinized cadence marching her toward an inevitable destination, the news suspended Mary, froze her in a sepia print permanently pasted in the scrapbook that would become the rest of her life. In June, Carlisle was closing. Its 14,000 days of loving destruction would end. The last of its 10,619 students were going home.

"Mary? Mary Moses?" The young man smiled at her, brown face earnest, his outstretched hand holding an envelope as if presenting himself for her formal consideration. She had noticed him standing beside the tracks, starched brown uniform in a pool of Indian shawls and moccasins, familiar sights at last as her train made its brief stop at the Spalding, Idaho, depot before hugging the Clearwater River home. Mary's raised eyebrows reflected her positive response, her smile accepting message and messenger alike. She recognized her father's handwriting penciled across this momentary bridge, this almost human touch, as the envelope passed between them.

Her father had taken a job with the Indian Agency, his printed words explained, and was living at Lapwai. He was sorry he could not greet her, but was away recruiting soldiers for the war. Their house was vacant. He had set up an account for her at the grocery store. He was not sure when he would be back in Kamiah. She should remember to go to church. The note was signed in longhand, *Billy Moses*.

A growing sadness accompanied Mary upriver, then gathered in puddles and dripped silently onto both cheeks as the train passed Agatha, Lenore, Peck, Orofino, and in between, empty milk cans beside the tracks like soldiers at attention.

Jimmy Girardoux sat beside her by the time the train had shuffled past Pardee. He carried her suitcase from the Kamiah depot to the wooden bridge across the river, where they chatted while two teams pulling wagons waited for Doc Ryan's Buick to finish its passage before starting their own. Jimmy walked behind her up the trail in the draw, past the garden of weeds to the empty house. They would meet that night, they decided, on the beach near the south end of the railroad bridge. They would welcome each other home.

He wrote to her from Georgia, *Oct. 10, 1918* stamped on the wrinkled envelope, script and print mixed on the page inside. He was ready, he wrote. Trained. Good at what he did. Eager to enter battle. Shipping out to France, he thought. He was a warrior. He knew he could never be killed by the enemy. He wished she could join him in a Quilloowaya song and dance, could give him moccasins for his journey. He did not have an address. That was all.

In mid-December, Kamiah lay gloomy in its valley, its streets bare, not a Christmas light in sight. The school was closed, churches dark, a 6:00 p.m. curfew the one rule that mattered. The influenza epidemic had found even this hidden part of the nation, mixing fever and pneumonia with quiet panic. Only the Odd Fellows Hall showed any activity, a temporary hospital in this still world, a single light bulb casting shadow on the helpers passing occasionally in or out of the building's narrow side door.

The news of the arrival of Jimmy Girardoux's body had swirled upriver from Lapwai like winter wind, had swept around East Kamiah and on to Mary's house with its squares of yellow light stitched on the hillside. Preparations must be made. The train would be met by warriors. The Seven Drums ceremony would be at sunrise.

A Christian girl, Mary did not walk behind the wagon across the bridge and through the fields to the pine-clad flat with granite stones amidst the grass. She would not attend the noonday feast that followed. Instead, she crossed the river on the railroad bridge, first light glistening the frost on the rails, black water flowing below, shore ice brittle on either bank. From its dead-limb perch on the south side of the river, an eagle watched her cautious steps from tie to tie. At the end of the bridge the tracks curved upstream. She arrived at the cemetery's edge just before the procession passed between the iron entrance gates, the two mules that pulled the wagon clouding the air with their breathing.

Mary knelt in dry needles near an old pine's trunk, not knowing whether she did so to pray or to hide, or both. Speakers faced the slanting sun edging along the eastern rim of the valley and offered words familiar as the seasons to this sacred ground, to the river nearby, the hills beyond. We come from the earth and are cared for by the earth and return to the earth, sang a man Mary had never seen before, a wide scar across his forehead. Others took up the song, voices rising in pitch, then hurtling down, down into guttural depths. When four men lowered the pine box into the freshly dug earth, Mary felt a kick, another confirmation of what her swelling belly had been telling her for weeks.

Four months later, she sat on the steps of her house in the midday sun, ribs sore, her belly in her lap. She was alive and not alone. She pressed her side, anticipating the response, and smiled. "Isaac is dancing," she said to a pine squirrel running along her porch rail.

She glanced toward the garden fence, the weeds filling the space inside, the hog wire gate hanging loosely from its hinges. She began to plan the rows, the hills, the beds, the angle of the water piped out of the creek to flow onto the eager earth. A glint of blue near the top of the garden gate focused her attention, caused her to rise and follow the path she had traveled as a child from house to garden and back. The patch of color stirred in a light breeze, then divided itself into two baby moccasins hanging from the top of the gate, blue beads on buckskin, softness wrapped in a faint smell of wood smoke.

CHAPTER FOUR

1952

Glass beads filled the top shelf of an antique oak display case facing the door of Uncle Bill's Pawn Shop—blue, red, orange and white on oval barrettes and bolo ties, key chains and a wallet beaded with the image of the American flag. The colors on the middle shelf were muted—soft tan of smoked deer hide, rich browns of otter fur, white ermine tails ending abruptly in their black tips. The bottom shelf looked heavy and gray with basalt mortars plowed from farmers' fields and granite pestles polished by the grip of generations. Real regalia—old, used, with the spirit still attached—were kept in the steel-grated back room awaiting word from a collector in Denver or Seattle or Santa Fe. Most items on display were the usual stock—what Isaac referred to as pow-wow cash—small crafts sold for a few dollars for a family visit or rodeo or pow-wow. He shuffled his boots on the worn wooden floor as he studied the pawn shop's contents like a hunter reading tracks, learning who had passed since his last visit to this discount bank for Indians where cash was traded for half-priced collateral which neither owner nor broker expected to be redeemed.

A second case, on Isaac's left, displayed four pocket watches, a variety of estate jewelry, a dozen or so elk ivories, and today a twenty-dollar gold piece shining through the polished glass like the front tooth of a grinning western gambler. Isaac smiled when he spied that coin. He didn't know what hand or circumstance had brought it here, but he did know that gold was about to change his life. In fact, it already had. His credit at the grocery store had once more been extended, though the *Lewiston Morning Tribune* headline "Nez Perces to Receive Gold Reparation Payments" hadn't yet softened the owner of the Boots & Saddles Bar. The U.S. government had announced that, starting in September, each member of the Nez Perce Tribe would receive a check from the Bureau of Indian Affairs for an estimated $1200 as payment for millions of dollars worth of gold extracted illegally from Nez Perce lands during the 1860's and '70's gold rushes. Gold fever was once more spreading across the valley floor.

"H'llo, Isaac. What do you have for me?" inquired 62-year-old Bill Sheffield flatly as he emerged from behind a row of rifles. He scanned this familiar customer, then raised his eyebrows in puzzlement over the smile he saw beneath Isaac's bangs and crooked nose.

"Whatcha give me for my chainsaw? A McCullough 150, runs good. You've had it here before."

"That saw's getting old, Isaac, and it's too small for loggers," came Uncle Bill's disinterested reply. "I'll give you fifteen bucks."

"It's got a new chain, and I'll get it back 'cause I need it this fall for making wood."

"You can't haul any wood with that broken-down pickup of yours. That thing hasn't run for at least two years. Why don't you keep the chainsaw and sell me your pickup. It's a '36, right?"

"'39, and it's not for sale. How about the chainsaw?" Isaac glanced at the gold coin again, tiring of this familiar exchange.

The pawnbroker rubbed a small scar on the right side of his jaw with his left hand, a gesture that often accompanied these financial negotiations. He studied Isaac's face, then his posture, searching for some clue that might guide him in his decision. "I'll give you twenty bucks and thirty days, and that's a deal."

"You loaned me twenty-five last time," Isaac responded, rubbing the toe of his boot against the dusty molding at the bottom of the showcase.

"I don't care what you're getting in that damned gold rush thing, Isaac. I've gotta make a living, and old McCulloughs aren't in much demand. Twenty bucks."

Isaac glanced once more at the twenty dollar gold piece just beyond his reach, suddenly wanting to smash the glass front, calmly pick up the shiny coin, give Sheffield a nod, and step next door for a drink. "I'll bring it in tomorrow," trailed behind him as he stepped through the pawnshop door. Squinting, he shaded his face with the bill of his cap and turned right toward the northern end of Main, midday sun hot on his back as he ambled toward the highway.

The first miners had arrived in Nez Perce country in 1860 and panned pay dirt 200 miles from the nearest white settlement at Walla Walla. The cry of *Gold!* soon echoed downstream, was swept along by the Columbia's unfettered flow to Portland, crossed the bar at Astoria and sailed to San Francisco. California, punched full of holes and teeming with hungry miners who hadn't seen much gold dust for a decade, flung whole towns north. This human wave flowed inland to the mouth of the Clearwater on 100-ton sternwheelers laden with picks and shovels, flour and hardtack, whiskey and pianos. On horses and mules and afoot, the miners stomped across the Nez Perce Reservation less than two years after the great white father in Washington had signed the treaty that guaranteed Nez Perce land "for the exclusive use and benefit of said tribe." By May of '61, 200 miners had staked claims along Canal Gulch high in the Clearwater Mountains. More soon shoveled rich ground along nearby Orofino Creek. By summer's end, 2000 people walked the hastily constructed Main Street of Pierce—miners, butchers, merchants and whores. Gamblers and gunmen streamed in like buzzards at a fresh kill, and greed became the fever of the day. Then the real white flood began.

When all the rich ground had been staked in the newly-formed Pierce and Orofino mining districts, gold-seekers panned their way past Nez Perce villages, followed trails and streams and dreams deeper into the reservation until fresh gold swirled in the panned black sands of the Clearwater's South Fork. Elk City storefronts were whipsawed into thin mountain air, and 3000 new miners spilled across the meadows like hungry badgers, digging their way into late autumn, thawing the ground with fires after freeze-up. Next, fabulous Florence was the district of choice, and a town of 6,000 hacked its way into the timber along Miller's Creek and Summit Flat, music from the hurdy gurdies often drowned out by nightly brawlings and occasional gunshots. Ninety years later a few ounces of gold dust were to trickle into Isaac's waiting hands.

The grill of Isaac's pickup grinned at the end of the grassed-in driveway to his house, the path tightly hedged by cottonwood shoots. Blackberry leaves lay thick on the top of the green Ford's cab and fenders, appliquéd with dew and mold and camouflaged among the patches of rust on the faded paint. Gold had been no stranger to Isaac in '49. Mill money from his first full-time job proved more than enough to buy a pickup with a bullet hole through the passenger's door—and as local newspapers reported, through the owner's hunting partner as well. An icon of painful memory, the Ford had been discounted for a quick sale. Now the truck stood entrapped in hardened vines as large around as Isaac's thumb, with inch-long thorns that could penetrate a Wallmont mule hide glove. He'd need to use his chainsaw before he took it to the pawnshop, Isaac concluded as he strode toward his porch carrying a bag of groceries purchased with a signature and a smile.

The following day Nick Snodderly's smile floated across the customer counter in the Texaco station at 6th and Main, just after he had scotch-taped another big buck photo face-up to the underside of the counter's glass top. "Whadya need, Isaac?" asked Nick, habitually wiping his grease-cracked hands with a soft pink cloth and then shoving the rag into a back pocket.

"I need to get my pickup running." Isaac glanced at parts and tools scattered across a workbench on the far side of the shop, wondering what combination might return his Ford to life. Nick's series of questions followed: how long had it been parked, how old was the battery, had he tried to start it, and so on, and with each reply Isaac tried to guess the cost and complications of the growing list of probabilities. "It's really pretty simple stuff with the '39s," came Nick's analysis. "You'll need a new battery, clean the sediment bowl, drain the gas tank and put in some fresh fuel. Then she'll probably fire up. Remember to check the tires and brakes before you drive it over here. Then we'll give it a good going over. Brake seals might be bad by now, happens when a rig just sits that long."

Isaac nodded his head with each pause in Snodderly's diagnosis, then grinned agreement with the final recommendation. "I need it for elk hunting this fall," Isaac declared, staring at the curly hair that crawled into the concave patch at the bottom of Snodderly's throat.

"How ya gonna pay for all that, Isaac?" Nick asked with a cautious tone. The two men talked about the gold reparation payments, about Nick's son and Isaac's former teammate, Danny, who was welding in Seattle, about the Winchester rifle that Isaac's uncle had given him years before. Isaac left the station with a used 6-volt battery and a 2-gallon can of Texaco regular. That evening he took a 3 x 5 ledger book from the top board of his kitchen shelves and in the light from a kerosene lamp added two more entries to the growing column of numbers and words.

Three days later he carried two new windows across the bridge from town, the hickory handle of the shiny hammer that filled his hip pocket rubbing the small of his back as he walked. A piece of cardboard soon curtained the newly installed window on the south side of the house. By evening the new slider on the west end just above Isaac's bed caught an upriver breeze filled with the sounds of owl and nighthawk. He had tried to add a cast iron woodstove to his list of purchases, but the store owner had stopped his credit with the windows despite the constant talk on Main about the money that would soon be flowing in the streets. Some merchants gambled freely, electing to absorb as much of the promised cash as possible before it arrived. Others approached the game more cautiously, covering their bets with increasing amounts of collateral.

Mid-October, Isaac extended his chainsaw chit at the pawnshop with $5 he got for three fall Chinook and a steelhead jack. He caught the fish with a short piece of gillnet a friend had given him the previous fall, putting the net out at night, pulling it at dawn, corks splashing at the top of the net the best part of his day.

Shaggymane mushrooms sprouted along the shoulders of the gravel road beside the river with the first fall frosts, then melted into inky spots as the whole town waited like gamblers for the turn of the next card.

When he filled two sacks with groceries the following week, Isaac could feel the merchants' patience draining away, worry stalking them like a threatening storm. A sign in the post office window summarized the situation. *No Checks* was printed in bold red letters. That evening he once more tallied his cashbook columns, confident now that all bets were placed, all players eager to see who would win, who would lose, which property would change hands once again.

The first Canadian cold front blew in skeins of geese and 4 inches of snow on Isaac's pickup sitting in the lot behind the Texaco station. The list of parts and labor had long exceeded the value of his Winchester, and Nick Snodderly had mentioned the possibility of a recovery sale. The pile of willow and cottonwood saplings Isaac had grubbed from his driveway in early autumn was now stove ash, along with the limbs and top of an uprooted fir he had axed stove-length and piled beneath his porch. In the shadowy chill of an early November afternoon, Isaac slid a folded piece of buckskin from beneath his bed and laid it on the end of the pine slab table that dominated the larger room of his cabin. He shivered as he laid each fold open, revealing a ledger book and an elkhorn quirt. The head of a beaver was etched into the wide end of the quirt's handle. Two strands of braided horsehair coiled from the other end. Their knotted tips fell towards the floor when Isaac gripped the quirt and lifted his right arm as if ready to whip a horse's flank behind him. Isaac ran the horsehair braids through his left hand, then laid the quirt full length along the table's edge.

The cover of the ledger book was tan and plain, book cloth threads worn smooth. Bound with linen, each of the 30 pages was marked horizontally by 15 blue lines crossed by 3 vertical lines in red. The front side of each page was blank but for these lines. Miniature portraits of children filled the backside of the pages, some penciled in black and intricate shades of gray, others in pastel greens, earthy reds, pale blues. Half the children had long braids wrapped with otter fur or black hair flaring above their shoulders, with bone chokers at their throats or shell earrings dangling above the beads and quill work that decorated their buckskin clothing. The remaining portraits depicted short-haired boys in high-collared uniforms and girls in gray woolen dresses. A few faces looked Nez Perce, the remaining portraits were of youth from other tribes, but all had large, quiet eyes, and all wore sadness like a shroud. Isaac's mother, Mary Moses, had found this ledger book in a crack in the stone wall back of Hatfield Hall at Carlisle Indian School in Pennsylvania, had tucked it into the top of her coarse wool dress, had hidden it beneath the stone bridge that arched over Letort Creek between the school and town. "This was Carlisle, Isaac," she said solemnly the evening before she left for Pendleton as she placed the ledger book in his hands like a sacred gift. "This is part of me," she added, wiping a tear from her right eye with the back of her hand. "Never leave your people, Isaac," she told him, "Don't ever leave your people."

Isaac took his own ledger book from his pocket and stared at the numbers he'd scribbled during the past three months. Windows, pickup, chainsaw, two boxes of .30-.30 shells, boots, a winter jacket, groceries, bar bill. He had added the columns over and over, each with the same result. He needed $692. He was out of wood. He was out of food. He was out of time.

He looked again at the column of figures. His right hand hardened around the handle of the quirt, then slowly relaxed as he placed the quirt carefully on its buckskin wrap and folded the soft hide around it. "A hundred dollars," he said firmly to himself as he put both ledger books in his jacket pocket, then stepped through his cabin door and walked slowly toward the river.

CHAPTER FIVE

1889

Sunlight flooded the open door of the two-room cabin, bounced off a sheet-steel stove and spread a soft glow over a two-foot square of thin rawhide that served as the only window on the south side of the building. Walking Woman stepped through the doorway and settled on the edge of a wooden porch, moccasins resting on the second of four plank steps that fell to a worn path down a narrow draw sloping toward the river. Summer surrounded her—the faded green of cottonwoods, brown hillsides climbing northward, dust deep in the wagon ruts above the river crossing.

For Walking Woman, this was a day of waiting, of wrapping her arms beneath her knees and rocking through the scenes she knew would find her. She was waiting for her husband to return from a meeting with the Measuring Woman. Walking Woman had seen this stranger four days earlier atop a wagon piled high with trunks, boxes and burlap-covered bags, part of the mystery of her presence. Another woman traveled with her, and the two had moved into the house by the church once home to Sue and Kate McBeth, Presbyterian missionaries to the Nez Perce. According to the stories rushing 60 miles upriver from the Indian agency at Spalding, the Measuring Woman had been sent by the government in Washington to draw more lines on the earth so that more fences could be built. She was explaining the new white man law in the church this very morning.

Walking Woman's garden fence already kept roaming livestock out of her beans and carrots, her squash and potatoes, and her house needed no separation from its surroundings. It was a fine house made of lumber sawed at the government mill two miles upriver from this wooded draw that coursed through higher benchland on either side. Daylight sneaked through hand-split shakes on the roof, but the hardest rain could not reach the polished puncheon floor. Moss and mud filled the cracks between the slabs of pine that sided the rough-cut framing, lumber the only pay her husband had ever received for weeks of guiding logs through whirling steel and stacking slabs of wood to dry in summer shade. She knew he was drawn to the mill site, the church, the sacred shadows in the house that had once been home to the McBeths. Walking Woman was a stranger there, the ground sucked dry of its spirit.

That church had gleamed a holy white the first time she had seen it from the ridgetop on the south side of the valley floor. She was Swan Feather then, a quiet sum of twelve summers. She remembered the horses, herded by the hundreds, her brother amongst the young boys chasing strays through the dusty confusion. She remembered mothers clucking to their children as they scurried downslope through dry bunchgrass and white-lichened basalt. But mostly she remembered that shining white church on the side of the river that meant safety from the noise of the cannons and rifle fire, from the smoke and cries and blood of battle. Her people had fled that day from the soldiers firing from high bluffs overlooking their village. Swan Feather had helped her mother, Speaks-in-Tongues, hurriedly pack two horses with what they could salvage from their lodge, had handed her baby brother to their mother's arms reaching out from her rawhide saddle. Swan Feather's own pony had skittered up a nearby slope, but stood its ground as she approached. Soldiers were entering the village by the time she rode past the warriors' rear guard, their faces peering from the rimrock like painted petroglyphs.

The next morning families had crossed the river in hastily made boats of willow and buffalo hide. She remembered Christian Nez Perces watching from the far shore, fearful of what their heathen relatives might bring upon them. With brown arms paddling bullboats and black-spotted ponies swimming the river and blue-coated soldiers cresting the ridge behind them, that church stood witness to what the white man's God had wrought upon the people who had sprung from the earth and the water and the blood of the monster slain by It'se-ye-ye here in this valley a long, long time ago.

Walking Woman needed to stand, to water her corn, to gather blackberries before the sun was high, but instead she kept traveling this haunting trail, visions layering their weight upon her. Sometimes she could turn away, could anchor herself in beadwork or basketry or in the soil and sun of her garden. But once she had mentally reached the Weippe Prairie and the ancient trail to the buffalo, she was inextricably pulled along steep ridges and pushed through deep mountain saddles, embedded in the scene of hundreds of Nez Perces jamming their horses across the tree-strewn trail, blood staining stumps and stobs behind them. Walking Woman closed her eyes, rocked slowly back and forth, and let the images carry her away.

At first the soldiers did not chase her people across the Bitterroots. On the other side of the mountains, Montana merchants sold them flour, beef and bacon. The people's pace slowed, over 700 men, women, boys, girls, babies and elders all finally feeling safe on their way to buffalo country. Only the voice of an old medicine man had shared a dream of danger and death.

They stopped to peel fresh lodge poles near the head of the Bitterroot River where lodgepole pine stood thick above the riverbank. The next day they crossed the divide and camped beside the Big Hole. They were safe and free, the Idaho soldiers far behind, and they danced into the night in celebration. This would be the last night Swan Feather would not feel alone.

The soldiers attacked in darkness, fired into lodges, fired at fleeing children, shot women in their beds. Swan Feather heard the guns and screams and ran into the river, wedged herself between a beaver house and the riverbank and shook, afraid to look at the glow of lodges burning in the first light of an unforgettable dawn. Her mother lay dead in a nearby ditch, baby limp at her side.

Walking Woman's rocking stopped as her left hand squeezed her right wrist, her belly tightened and a series of shudders rippled through her. When they ended, the rocking returned and a new collage of scenes continued to mark her journey.

She didn't remember where they had gone after they buried their dead at the Big Hole. Every day seemed the same—eat what could be found, pack, ride, unpack, cook, eat, sleep. Some days there was fighting, others none. Some days there was food, others none—but always the move, the run.

The final battle, near the Bear Paw Mountains, lasted five days. Here Swan Feather huddled cold and still in a cave she helped dig in the side of a ravine by scraping away the sandy soil with a digging stick and cooking pan as canon shot and rifle fire flew overhead. By the second day they had no wood. On the fourth day, snowfall and a steady wind buried the dead around them in drifting shrouds. Her father, Two Crows, lay among the mounds slowly disappearing into the landscape.

A horse and rider appeared on the wagon road below Walking Woman's house and turned up the side trail toward the porch on which she sat frozen in the sunshine. She squinted, attempting to identify her visitor. The gait of the horse and the cradleboard hanging from the saddle told her the rider was her friend Little Otter. The gelding stopped a few feet away, familiar with the routine. The two women visited about Little Otter's baby, the women at the missionary house, the meeting at the church, fall root digging on the Weippe Prairie. Then the visitor kneed her horse out of the yard toward her mother-in-law's house on the first bench overlooking the river, her visit a brief dream dropped between the scenes of real life at the Bear Paw once more flooding Walking Woman's mind.

On the afternoon of the fifth day, the fighting stopped. Women and children emerged from their shelters and clustered around narrow columns of smoke, unable to wait for wet willow to dry into flame. Her brother found her at dusk. A jagged tear across his forehead had trailed blood down the side of his face. He was leaving that night, he told her, would slip past the soldiers picketed around them, would make a run north to Grandmother's Land. No, she would not join him, could not join him, she tried to explain, her mind as numb as her body, her spirit flat, her only feeling the pain of her frostbitten fingers thawing in the choking smoke.

On the sixth day the people buried their frozen dead and were ushered along their own trail toward dying. Over 400 in number, flanked by even more soldiers, they walked and rode, on horseback and in wagons—three children for every woman, two women for every man, and Swan Feather, alone. Neither woman nor child, she had walked whenever she could, finding an unexpected peace in step after step through the nothingness that stretched from days into weeks, always farther and farther from home. At the Bearcoat General's fort, women and children were loaded onto flatboats. Spray froze on the rails as they huddled in the fog of their own breath, the general's promise of their return to their homeland growing weaker with every Yellowstone River rapid and bend of the Missouri, vanishing completely as they boarded rail cars in Bismarck, North Dakota. As the train bore east, Swan Feather felt she had died on some unknown ridge or riverbank or in some lonely coulee or canyon behind them.

Then all around her the real dying returned. At first, death came from wounds of the body, then from wounds of the heart—first from the intolerable cold, then from the ravishing heat. Dumped as refuse upon barren land in the middle of a Kansas winter, 21 Nez Perce died by spring. Later that year the forlorn living escaped the malarial swamp that emerged from the thawing ground around them, once again leaving their dead behind. Graves were easier to dig for the 47 more who died during the group's first Oklahoma autumn.

At *Eeikish Pah*, the hot place, even the babies died. Birth after birth, the trail to the sagebrush flat at the edge of the village became worn and familiar.

In her nineteenth spring the exile ended, and Swan Feather rode a train car west unsure of who she was or where she was going. At Wallula beside the Snake River the rail line ended, and five days later, she and 117 other survivors rode into Spalding, Idaho, and turned their mounts up Lapwai Creek. An Indian Fourth of July spread before them, the blending of an ancient Nez Perce summer celebration with an American tradition first shared with them by trappers and traders. The Christian Nez Perces camped on the west side of the creek, bolstering their righteousness with song and Psalm. The heathens held forth across the creek on a flat large enough for horse racing, gambling and dancing. From the east side, cheers and wails and drums greeted the exiles. The west bank was silent. In Oklahoma the Nez Perce had been one people in a faraway land. Here they were two people divided by a creek and two spirit women, Kate and Sue McBeth, who drew invisible lines between husbands and wives, relatives and friends.

Walking Woman's mental journeys always ended on that day on Lapwai Creek, as if the four years of her life since then were a gauzy mist the sun could not lift from the valley floor. This she knew: Swan Feather had become Walking Woman, had married, had moved to this house where she now sat on the top step of the front porch in the sunshine waiting for a new dawn to emerge from the darkness that haunted her like an owl's cry in the night.

The whites are always making lines, thought Walking Woman—between Indians and whites, between Indians and Indians, between Indians and their land. Her husband would return soon from the meeting Measuring Woman had called to tell the Indians what new fences the government would build, who would be kept out, who kept in, what families would be divided, what peoples destroyed. Would this house be hers or someone else's house? Where would her children live one day? Would she and Billy Moses have children, or would the fence between them grow thick as stone, heavy as a monster's heart? Walking Woman rocked slowly back and forth and waited.

CHAPTER SIX

1952

On Friday, November 17th, long-awaited nuggets of Nez Perce gold trickled out of Canal Gulch, Newsome Creek and American Meadows and arrived in Kamiah in the form of U.S. Government warrants, one of which had *Isaac Moses* printed in fine red dots on its pale gray background. As if acknowledging this anxiously awaited day, the sun had cracked a layer of clouds in early afternoon, luring Isaac from his shaded cabin to sunshine on the riverbank. He lingered there admiring the patience of a great blue heron standing motionless in a backeddy waiting for that moment when predator and prey intersect and time quickens in its circle. Jimmy Lean Elk shouted the news from the cab of his pickup, waving an envelope through its windowless door, as Isaac tracked the sound of tires on gravel and the heron struck.

Back at his cabin, he gathered his props. He had rehearsed this day for weeks, a jumble of financial figures, pawn shop dates, and sardonic smiles all rolled into script, timing and costume—with scenes as detailed as the drawings in his mother's ledger art book and sounds as fine as a Ford engine idling smoothly on a winter's day. His was the lead performance, and he had practiced his lines well. Act I would be triumph, followed by flashes of warm fires and winter elk, beer, laughter and respect.

The temperature began dropping as he crossed the highway bridge to town. Cars filled both sides of Main. People had gathered in front of the post office, and the line for general delivery spilled onto the sidewalk. He joined the festive crowd, smiled, visited, watched the hands of the Westlock clock on the post office wall move toward 3:40, 3:45, then disappear behind him as he inched through the inner door and waited for his turn at the counter.

The clock read 3:54 when Isaac returned to the street and angled towards the bank. Scene 2 was easy—a casual stroll across Main, then Fifth with a growing grin, four steps under the arch that framed the entrance to the Idaho First National Bank, and cash stacked before him on the marble countertop. The bank's 4:00 p.m. closure required an adjustment in his plan. He cut diagonally across the intersection, double-stepped the concrete stairs, then grinned at the chubby bank clerk crossing the lobby to lock up for the day. Once inside, his only line was "$20s and $50s", a compromise between substantiality and efficiency. He smiled again at the clerk as she unlocked the door for his exit, his left hand pressed against the fresh bulge in his jacket pocket. Streetlights were blinking on as he returned to street level, one illuminating the Texaco star on its metal pole above the gas pumps across Main. Isaac stepped eagerly into Scene 3.

The gas station lobby was quiet except for the buzz of a bare fluorescent light directly over the brass cash register that displayed a $5.00 sale, a full tank of gas complete with 50 green stamps to be licked and pasted into the premium books hidden in every purse and glove box in town. The smell of new rubber from the tire display bumped against the odor of grease from the lube rack visible through the open door to the shop. The distinctive *kachunk* of an air compressor feeding a pneumatic grease gun told Isaac that the station attendant was lubing the last car of the day and that Nick Snodderly had likely left work early to attend the football game in Cottonwood.

"I'm here for my pickup," Isaac announced to the freckled face that greeted him from beneath a '49 Plymouth suspended overhead. "I'm in kind of a hurry," he added as the high school boy reluctantly wiped the grease from his hands on a paper towel and glanced at the Pepsi clock on the wall whose minute hand approached 20 and pointed to the bare right breast of a leggy blonde on a tattered poster above a pile of spent batteries.

"Uncle Nick told me you might be in. He said not to give you any keys until you paid up."

"You find the bill and we'll make that cash register sing," Isaac responded, pleased with this ad-libbed line.

The young man followed him into the front section of the station. Greasy fingers thumbed through a stack of work orders while Isaac counted out 3 fifties and a twenty on the dirty glass countertop between them. "I'll take the extra $3.60 in gas," Isaac announced as the boy slid two pages of inky smudge in his direction.

Isaac's satisfaction was unrehearsed. He shoved the folded work order into his shirt pocket and left the cardboard tag attached to his keys, *Isaac* scrawled in red pen across its greasy surface. He quickly rounded the corner of the stucco building and tracked through shallow snow to the corner of the back lot. After wiping the snow off the driver's side windshield with his coat sleeve, he coaxed the stiff door lock into turning and slid into the final take of Scene 3 in full anticipation of pulling up in front of Uncle Bill's Pawn Shop just two blocks away. Choke out, he pumped the gas pedal three times, then eagerly turned the key. The starter shook and turned over, groaned four times, and quit. A clicking sound on second try confirmed that the battery beneath the snow-covered pickup hood was dead.

Bobby was lowering the hoist in the lube room when Isaac thrust his face through the doorway. "My battery's dead," Isaac announced, staring directly at the freckles that marched up both sides of Billy's nose like tiny ladybugs. "I need a jump."

"I gotta get this car out, and we're closing at 5. Big game on the prairie, you know. And you'll need a good overnight charge on that battery anyway. You could grab a wrench and a battery strap and bring it in for me. We're open at 8:00."

Isaac looked again at the pile of dead batteries along the far wall, glanced up shaved legs to the bikini bottom barely large enough to hold the word *Eveready* embroidered across its front panel, passed by the bare breasts and stopped at the clock, which now read 4:37. "I have to go right now." He poked the words in Bobby's direction. "If you don't get to it tonight, put that battery on charge first thing in the morning. Okay? I'll pick it up later in the day. And remember the gas you owe me." The young man gave a noncommittal nod as Isaac slid his pickup keys into his pocket and lurched through the front door.

A crowd still filled the sidewalk by the post office, so he crossed Main to the east side of the street and headed north, quickly passing the meat market and hardware store. Across Fourth the sign for the Boots and Saddles Bar angled obliquely toward the center of town from the building's beveled corner. He could hear the jukebox as he strode past, Hank Snow still movin' on. His pace slowed, his pulse quickened, and he was reaching for the porcelain knob on the pawn shop door when he saw a hand-scrawled note in the window posted just above the weekly hours of business: *Monday through Saturday, 10:00 to 5:00.* Scribbled in red crayon on a piece of paper torn from a grocery sack and scotch-taped to the glass, the note said *Closed till Monday.* Isaac read the note twice. He shaded his eyes with his right hand and stared through the pawnshop window, past the glass cases illuminated by a single light and on to the steel-grated door at the back of the room that guarded the walk-in safe. His mind raced through the script of his drama searching for lines, the pawn ticket prop, and the cue for his contemptuous smile. His left arm shook as he pulled his wallet from his hip pocket and retrieved two pawn tickets. His throat tightened as his eyes squinted at the date he knew so well, black ink on white cardstock, *November 18, 1952.* The shaking in his arm rippled through his chest and traveled to the sidewalk like an electric current finding ground. With wandering steps he started back toward the center of town, *Dry Goods And Groceries* providing a distant glimpse of Scene 5, when the voice of Kitty Wells pulled him off the street like a lodestone as the curtain fell and a long night began.

Cigarette smoke floated above a stained linoleum floor as Isaac stepped into the surging celebration at the Boots and Saddles Bar. The actual bar separated the laughing crowd from rows of bottles mounted on shelves like trophies, overhead lights illuminating the familiar names Jim Beam, Seagrams Seven, and Wild Turkey. A hint of cheap perfume layered the sour smell of stale beer and cigarette butts that saturated the knotty-pine walls accented by dusty deer heads and the cattle brands of local ranches.

Isaac fell into a chair at an empty table for two just inside the entrance by the bar's only window. The light from a street lamp blurred through the oily film on the windowpane. Dead flies lined the grooves at the bottom of the window's aluminum frame. Words and numbers and faces flashed inside his head, and he tried to slow their spin, to read the script, to find some quiet water, some solid ground.

"Hey, Isaac. Whatcha havin' tonight? Danny says the first drink's free if you pay your bar bill. He saw ya in the post office. Anything you want, even a beer and a bump." Cindy smiled, her stained teeth brown against the wisps of bleached hair she brushed behind her ear. "What'll ya have, Isaac?"

Isaac slid his left hand into his jacket pocket and rolled his fingers over the folded bills. The spinning in his head slowed, then stopped at $88.00 and the last time he had sat on one of the Naugahyde barstools and assured Danny he would have a check any day. He peeled two bills from the outside of the roll and handed them to Cindy, the streetlight confirming the keeping of his promise. "I'll have a boilermaker. Give me ten in credit, and you keep two bucks for your smile." Cindy took the two fifties, nodded toward Danny, and disappeared into the eager crowd. She returned with a shot and a beer chaser. "It's gonna be a great night, Isaac. Keep it fun," she admonished. Cold Bud soon chased Jim Beam heat down Isaac's throat.

The thwack of a breaking cue ball startled him, focused him once more on the slowly turning numbers in his head, the wad of cash in his pocket, his pickup covered with snow, the ledger art book in the pawn shop just beyond the bricks that formed the back wall of the bar. His breathing quickened, his thick hands formed into fists, fingernails pressed hard against his palms.

When the cue ball struck again, Isaac stood, crossed Cindy's trail as she approached the bar for the next round. Everyone smiled as he weaved through the crowded tables to the men's room. A bare light bulb hanging from the ceiling washed the walls a dirty yellow. Isaac slid the metal bolt on the door into the hole in the door casing, lowered the toilet lid and sat. The plastic creaked under his weight. He unlaced his left boot and pulled it from his foot, his right wrist hitting the snoose-stained urinal filled with the odor of old piss. He peeled seven twenty-dollar bills from his cash supply, stuffed them into the bottom of his boot, and mentally filed the hardware bill of $129.85 as he pulled the leather laces tight and knotted his determination. The right boot was next, four twenties for the grocery store, three more for boots and jacket, two fifties for the ledger art, another fifty for chainsaw and change. He stood, moved to the urinal, unzipped and peed, chasing three cigarette butts around the bottom of the porcelain bowl. A glance at the wall before him revealed a fist-sized hole in the sheetrock, its white edge the only fresh surface in the room. Isaac measured its size with his own large fist, rough brick rubbing his knuckles. In the upper left corner of his reach he felt a crevice between two bricks. He rolled four fifties into a tight cylinder and slid them into that crack, the ends protruding just enough for fingernails to grip and pull. He shoved the remaining bills into his left pants pocket, slid the bolt on the bathroom door and strolled back into a thickening haze.

By 9:00 p.m. twangy strings had yielded to a pounding beat. Small groups flowed in from the frosty night and took the scene's pulse, measured the beat and twist, and when these matched their own they stayed, adding energy to the room and a fresh round of drinks for the house. The arteries in the bartender's face turned brighter red as he stuffed more bills into a bank deposit bag, zipped the canvas closed and slid it under his coat beneath the bar beside the snub-nosed .38 he kept for special occasions.

Isaac cradled his head in his hands, elbows propped on the tabletop by the window near the front door after his third migration through the crowd of acquaintances and a gradual retreat to the lonely edge. He had pitched himself through the usual stages of fun and anger, pity and pain. Now energy drained from his pores like sweat, dripped down his arms and legs and disappeared onto the dance floor. He stared at the snowflakes falling through the muted light of the street lamp, thought about the tracks he would make in the fresh snow up the draw between his house and the river, tried to wish his cabin warm. Arctic air stung his face as he stepped through the front door and spilled onto the street.

A battered pickup swerved toward the east side of Main, its right front tire scraping the curb as it slid on the fresh snow. "Hey Isaac." Jimmy Lean Elk grinned through the passenger door of his pickup. "Get in, man. I'm headin' upriver. They've got some new broads at the Kooskia Inn. Good lookin' ones I hear. Let's go check it out."

CHAPTER SEVEN

1889

Billy Moses rode troubled down the draw from his two-room house, the gray of its weathered siding the same shade as the fog settled stubbornly along the riverbank where the trail met the wagon road to East Kamiah. The crisp white of his long-sleeved shirt contrasted sharply with his black, buttoned vest. Straight black hair touched the shirt's collar. His pants matched the vest, and morning dew beaded on the toes of his polished boots. Needing time to think about the coming event in his life, he let his bay set a casual pace.

He had traveled this same route the day before, a Sunday, and every Sunday morning for the past two years. The road paralleled the river, then curved past a forty-foot high mound of black basalt rising abruptly from the valley floor—the heart of the monster slain long ago by It'se-ye-ye, Coyote. From the body parts of this monster, It'se-ye-ye had created all but one of the Native tribes of North America. Reminded by Fox that he had failed to create any two-leggeds for the Clearwater Valley, It'se-ye-ye had washed his bloody paws in a basket of water from the river and sprinkled the ground, and from each drop of blood and water touching earth, up sprang a Nimiipuu, a Nez Perce, a people with good hearts sharing forever this place and this beginning.

A half-mile upriver the whitewashed steeple of the First Presbyterian Church pointed boldly toward the heaven of the Christian God. In the beginning, the missionaries said, this God had created a man and a woman and a snake, and all of the man and woman's children and their children's children were born in sin and had to ask forgiveness for the evil within them. Billy had been baptized in this church, water from the river washing away the darkness that would otherwise be with him forever.

He and his wife, Walking Woman, had attended services in the church the previous day. The congregation had listened to the Reverend Williams speak of God in the Nez Perce tongue. They had read a Psalm and sung a hymn, well practiced in the ritual and rhythm they had been learning for sixteen years. Walking Woman had sat silently throughout the service, her buckskin dress draped like a carving in yew or maple among the calicos that blossomed from the faded blue benches. She had watched the children sitting quietly on the platform at the front of the church, their small brown hands folded in their laps. At the end of the service her eyes had followed the wide black skirt of the woman swishing up the narrow aisle. Once on the alter platform, the woman had turned toward them, removed her bonnet, and looked at her audience with soft brown eyes in a round white face. She was Measuring Woman. She was the government agent who had been driven out of Lapwai by the heathens and had arrived in Kamiah with the blessings of Sue McBeth, long-time missionary to the Kamiah Nez Perce. Measuring Woman announced that she had been sent by the government in Washington to give the Nez Perces land and make them Americans. She told them of a meeting the following day at the church to talk about land and citizenship for all the Indians.

The members of the First Presbyterian Church did not visit about their usual after-church topics as they lingered beneath the limited shade of the young Ponderosas near the church's front steps. The quality of the huckleberry crop or promise of the fall salmon run had given way to this new development in their collective lives, this woman who had come to give them land, to steal their land; to make them citizens, to destroy their tribe.

Billy had watched his wife march down the church steps and cut through the crowd with a rapid stride, the anger in her eyes a match for the gaze of a wrathful god. She seldom rode her piebald home, preferring her feet on the earth and the rhythm of her own gait. He knew that for the rest of the day there would be no conversation between them, no glances his way. Food would appear on their table as if prepared by a shadow. Her evening would be spent in the garden, silently shucking beans and stirring the shells on the ground with her bare toes. After two years together, his wife remained a mystery.

This morning Billy once more followed the ruts in the road that meandered around a blackberry thicket as if understanding the futility of confronting such determination. With the familiar destination of the church growing near, his horse quickened its pace until he reined it in a short distance from the mission house, just outside the split rail fence that defined the edges of a barren yard. Here in this house Billy had held his mother's hand and heard the story of Jesus, had played in the yard with other children while their mothers learned from Kate McBeth how to sew cotton and can fruit, and Kate's sister Sue taught Nez Perce men how to preach and pray and drive evil from the land. His mother had joined Kate's class the year his father was sent to Lapwai to be cured of the coughing disease. Blood splattered on a pressed white shirt was Billy's only memory of his father's departure. The McBeths had insisted he needed a white man's cure, pointing to the ineffectiveness of the local medicine man as proof of their position. Billy never saw his father again.

For the past five years the mission house sat empty, windows closed, board and batten siding blending with the morning fog that frequented the valley. Now two new white women had appeared—the measuring woman and her cook-companion—here to preach a new message about land and citizenship. Their wagon stood in the yard. A wooden water bucket sat at the top of the steps leading to the house's only door. Billy nudged his mare forward, trying to read this special place, to smell and feel its spirit.

When he arrived at the church, more than three-dozen men stood visiting outside the door, brown skin the major color amongst their black and white attire. Someone rang the bell mounted at the rear of the church, its heavy tones circling the building's clapboard sides. The men filed silently inside and took their places on the benches that filled much of the room lit only by rectangles of sunlight from the four windows on the church's east side. Blue cloth glued to the walls had faded unevenly into a mosaic of muted texture. The ceiling was painted blue, as was the pulpit standing on a platform two steps high at the far end of the room. The men stared implacably at Measuring Woman as she walked up the aisle as if to deliver a sermon. The second step to the platform squeaked beneath her, and then she stood at the pulpit with her interpreter at her side. She spoke with a calm voice, stopping frequently so her message could be translated into the Nez Perce tongue.

"My friends, this is God's house and what we are to talk about is a serious matter affecting the lives and happiness of all—your lives, and the lives of your wives and children. It is right to ask God's blessing here in this house, that all we do may please Him."

Billy felt safe in this church where he had often sat as a boy with his mother and listened to Sue McBeth speak of love and joy and saving grace. Now another woman promised from the pulpit that he could become a citizen and have his own land and fencing and one day money to buy cattle, a wagon and maybe even glass windows for his house. She spoke with quiet confidence while beams of sunlight traveled up the pulpit's stem and onto her gesturing hands and earnest face. At the end of her speech she thanked them for coming and asked them to consider her words carefully. Billy sat motionless, his eyes fixed on that smiling face speaking now with Reverend Williams near the pulpit while most of the men filed out of the church. Billy finally stood, then walked past grumbles on the front porch steps, past talk of the "steal treaty" of '63 and the government fencing on Indian lands consistently ignored by white ranchers and settlers.

He decided to take the long way home, needing time to consider the words he had heard, this promise not of inheriting the earth in the life hereafter but of having the good life now, in this time and this place, for himself and his wife and for the children he hoped they would have one day. If the mill would start up again, he could get lumber and build a new house and barn on the land the government would give him. As the head of a household, he would get 160 acres. A child would add another 40 acres. He could have fields of grain and pasture for a cow. He would choose his land close to the mill and the church and the river. His wife could learn English and grow a bigger garden and smile in church and learn to pray.

He reined his horse to a stop near the mission house. The windows were open now, top sash down and bottom sash up, the way they had been when he had listened to the music from a cabinet organ float out of the house and over the landscape. Leaving playmates behind in the rocky yard, he would often walk to the house and sit beneath the window closest to that sound, content to wait for his mother inside learning to pray and sew like white women. Today his gaze shifted from the open windows to a woman watching him from the porch steps. Her penetrating eyes appeared almost black beneath blond curls and darker brows. Her skirts covered the bottom two steps and touched the ground before her. A writing board spanned her thighs, filling her lap to the knees. After a studied stare at Billy, she continued her writing.

> *She tells them she has come to bring them manhood, that they may stand up beside the white man in equality before the law. The idea is hard to grasp. The prospect of standing beside the white man is not a very brilliant one. The unadulterated Indian looks down upon the species of white men he knows anything about. As to the law, all they know about the law is that it is some contrivance to get ponies and cattle and land out of the red man's possession into that of the white man; it is a one-sided machine; it never brings back an Indian's stolen horse, or takes the border ruffian's fence or his cattle off the Indians' land.*

Billy kneed his horse toward the river, then paused beside a single-carriage sawmill and nearby stack of pine logs rotting in the sun. As a boy of eight he had watched his father pull logs to the mill from the nearby hills with a team of horses, had seen the yellow slabs fall from the shiny blade and be stacked in the shade to dry. At 18 he had stood his turn feeding red fir to the whirring teeth, piling boards the color of a martin's back. He dismounted, crossed ground spongy from rotted sawdust and sat on the edge of the mill's hand-hewn deck. The steady stare of the woman at the mission house lingered, and he thought as well about the Measuring Woman and Sue and Kate McBeth and his mother all at this place, in that church and in that house, looking at him and pointing the way to salvation. It was the sixth woman in his life that perplexed him, the woman who would not separate earth and sky, Christians and Dreamers, heaven and hell.

He had been at this very spot twelve years earlier when he first saw the non-treaty Nez Perces pouring into the valley from the ridges across the river. The entire mountainside seemed to be moving, a slow-motion avalanche of people and ponies. These non-Christian Dreamers had been fighting with the soldiers, he knew, but suddenly they were here, more than seven hundred, with two thousand horses. Warriors had splashed across the river and fanned out amongst the pine trees, and one rode directly past the mill. Billy had smelled the sweat from the running horse and had seen the black paint streaked down the warrior's face. With a single glance at Billy, the warrior was gone, but Billy remembered those eyes, the painted face, the blood caked on the man's leg pressed against the horse's heaving side.

The next day the women and children and old men crossed the river in buffalo hide boats hurriedly made on gravel bars, boys driving the horse herd and warriors bringing up the rear. In small groups the non-treaties had filed past these same trees, past the mill and mission house, the church and the lodges of their treaty relatives. Concealing himself beneath the sawmill deck, Billy had watched the long parade for much of the afternoon, especially the children who walked silently by their mothers' sides. Later he learned that one of the young girls he likely saw that day was Swan Feather—Walking Woman—who waited now for him to bring the news of what she would view as the latest white man's scheme to take their land, their livelihood, their lives.

Walking Woman had been his last temptation in her quiet way. Three years earlier, the Fourth of July celebration had brought together the Christians and the Dreamers in one big camp, a plan sold to the missionaries by the Indian agent as a means for the Christian Nez Perces to influence their unruly brethren. The missionaries recognized this arrangement would also eliminate their annual efforts, often unsuccessful, to keep Christ's flock from slipping away to the heathens' celebration and the consequences such transgressions required. Billy had once been one of those transgressors and had been granted forgiveness only because of his youth and the sincerity of his confession.

Amidst prayers and singing, drums and dancing, with the chants of the stick games drowning out the most fervently sung hymns, Billy had watched Walking Woman add her voice to *Quilloowaya*, the song for departing warriors. She had emerged from the darkness as the singing began, irresistibly drawn to the sadness in the women's voices as each took a position in the circle directly behind her chanting lover. Walking Woman had remained on the edge of the circle, bobbing with the rhythm, her voice the loneliest sound Billy had ever heard. Later he had seen her sitting alone, a mute observer, a shadow in the evening light. She watched his approach neither shyly nor invitingly, but smiled when he sat beside her. In the courtship that followed he learned she was a Dreamer and had been in the war. A year later they were married in the First Presbyterian Church now passing out of sight behind him.

He passed the trail to his house, puffs of dust rising from each track his mare made in the August earth. Drifting now in his own aimless current, he continued downstream through the cottonwoods that lined the river's bank. A thin column of smoke on the opposite bank rose from a narrow strip of sand. A small hut of bent willows and blankets squatted near the fire. The old tewat is getting ready for more mischief, thought Billy, echoing the line he had heard so often from the McBeths as they turned their followers away from the traditional medicine men of the tribe. Billy had never heard the hiss of water on hot rocks or plunged his steaming body into the icy flatness of a November eddy. He had learned well that Christians cleansed themselves with pious prayer and store-bought soap.

A mile downstream the trail left the river and crossed a grassy flat. He made no protest as his horse nibbled toward a circle of stone rising 3 feet above the ground and 30 feet across, the remains of an ancient pit house. A single Ponderosa grew inside its center, the trunk nearly the size of Billy's thigh. He studied the circle, each rock placed by ancestors centuries before. For a moment he wanted to touch those rocks, to stand within the circle, to search for a message on the pine-needle floor. Instead, he turned his horse toward home.

Walking Woman offered no greeting from the porch as he rode into the yard. She shifted her position to the top of the steps and watched him unsaddle his horse. He took off his broad-brimmed hat and sat on the second step below her, hoping her arms would find his shoulders, his neck, the top of his chest under his unbuttoned shirt, but she neither touched him nor spoke.

"We can get 160 acres," Billy finally began, abandoning various strategies he had considered on the final leg of his morning's journey. "And 40 acres for any children."

"We have no children," stated Walking Woman flatly.

"It will be our own land, and we can become citizens," he added cautiously.

"Where will we dig our roots and graze our ponies?" Walking Woman's voice was etched in anger. "Where will we set our fish traps and hunt game and gather wood?"

Billy knew the futility of arguing with bitterness and non-belief.

"What land will our children have, and our children's children? And their children after them?" Walking Woman stood, looking down on her husband's upturned face, her tone biting, accusing. "If you trust the white man, you are a fool!" She disappeared into the silence of their cabin.

"We have no children!" His angry words followed her through the open doorway. He rose, wanting to get away from this woman, this anger, this painful wound in his life. Instead he walked up the stairs, through the doorway, and started to shake.

Walking Woman understood pain. She knew it stronger than sorrow, deeper than love. Her hands found her husband's face, his tight neck, his heaving shoulders. She led him to the bed in the shadowed end of their two-room house, to the one place they shared in their otherwise separate lives. It was here they had found warmth if not love, caring if not passion, a place to forget if not to forgive. They each knew the fences would come, on the land and in their lives, but for this moment the dim glow of sunlight from their house's rawhide windows was the only thing that needed to be between them.

CHAPTER EIGHT

1952

Isaac needed a ride, Jimmy needed a friend, and the two young men set out to carve a hole in the winter night. Cowboy music from K-O-R-T and cold air blasting through the windowless passenger door of Jimmy's pickup made contemplation more practical than conversation. Recalling Jimmy's mention of the new barmaids at the Kooskia Inn seven miles upstream, Isaac closed his eyes and recalled the rounded butts in tight blue jeans balanced on the stools at the Boots and Saddles Bar he had stumbled out of minutes before. The glow of Kamiah's streetlights melted away as Jimmy turned east at the end of the bridge over the Clearwater River. He braked once for a spike buck losing traction on the slick pavement, deer and pickup each leaving skid marks in the half inch of snow that covered the highway. Ten minutes later Jimmy shifted into third, slipped a corner and pulled onto a steel-arched bridge, its crossbars battered by logging trucks with too high a load. The first river ice of the season edged the Middlefork beneath the highway light that announced Kooskia's tattered entrance. The tipi burner at Cory's mill glowed rusty red, testimony to another shift of logs slabbed into boards while the smoke from burning bark and sawdust poured into the sky.

The dark red brick of the Kooskia Inn suggested a quality that had long disappeared—a bank perhaps, or fine restaurant. Now the bricks sloughed rotting mortar, and a *No Caulks* sign on the entrance door belied the hole-punched path from door to bar that logger's boots laid to the first beer at the end of a 12-hour day. Jimmy led, foolishly oblivious of the fact that he and Isaac would likely be the only Indians in the bar, curiosity ahead of caution, hubris as strong as hormones. Isaac followed. A rectangular patch of light illuminated the green felt of a pool table just inside the door. A shock of gray hair tilted back from the far side of the table's edge, then passed out of the light as a grin with yellowed teeth, two missing, shined toward the newcomers. A single eye focused on the chosen ball, the stroke, the hit. The grin returned with the sound of a ball dropping into a side pocket and the groans of the two other players at the table.

Jimmy and Isaac slipped into the first empty booth, past two young loggers in bobbed canvass pants and Romeos. Three men sat in the corner booth laughing loudly. Two more claimed the far end of the bar. At the near end, two women on barstools flashed a greeting with fishnetted thighs and warm smiles above red blouses V'd in invitation. The older woman flowed across the room, bent low over the newcomers' table, and asked in a soft voice what Jimmy and Isaac would like to drink. She walked slowly back to the bar with their order, measuring the glances that followed her from the shadows surrounding the pool table. Isaac watched her return with their beers, his eyes gliding from chest to thighs and back. He traced the curve of her hips as she checked the other booths, then returned to her perch like a hawk waiting for fresh rustling in a newly mowed hay field.

The two friends talked: the steelhead run and winter hunts and the comparative physical merits of the two women at the bar, one soft and friendly, the other leggy and flat. Jimmy was thinking about going to Haskell, he told Isaac, of learning a trade, though Kansas seemed a long way off. A window for his pickup was going to cost 20 bucks. His cousin was getting married and buying a car. The friendly barmaid would feel so good moving beneath his hips. He signaled for another round.

The two loggers were the first to leave, frozen ground guaranteeing a 5 a.m. departure for another day of felling trees and limbing and bucking logs. Soon after, the loudest of the three in the corner booth wobbled to the door assisted by the slender barmaid, cold air sweeping into the room as the door slammed shut behind them. The pair at the far end of the bar stayed hunched together, the wide-faced man with rounded shoulders gliding whisky down his throat half shot glass at a time, then smoothing any rough spots with tap beer. Three full bottles of Bud stood neatly queued in front of the younger man, his curly head bobbing out words he read from a notebook between names the two exchanged with smiles—Roethke and Rilke and others who Isaac knew did not live at Woodland or Winona or any of the other tucked away townships that dotted the edge of the prairie.

It was nearly midnight when Luella slid into Jimmy's and Isaac's booth and stayed. Her right leg rubbed Jimmy's calf; her right arm snaked around the small of his back. She lit a Marlboro and slid an ashtray past the change from a twenty still piled in the center of the table. For a brief time Isaac enjoyed her scent, her curves scribing arcs in the dim light, the occasional smile she tossed his way. When she and Jimmy slipped farther into the corner of the booth and began to giggle, Isaac stood, crossed the room and slumped onto the stool closest to the row of uncapped Buds creeping down the bar. At the other end of this tall-necked row, the curly-headed sipper read from his notebook "nothing dies as slowly as a scene." The gulper looked down the bar and photographed Isaac's face with a searching gaze, then turned his attention once more to the words his friend poured freely between them. Isaac took the nearest Bud in his left hand, quietly slid it down the bar to his right and swiveled clockwise on the barstool to the sound of the tavern door clicking closed. The pool table lay silent. The plastic Coca-Cola shade above the felt squeezed light toward the triangle of painted balls racked in place waiting for the next slice of skill or chance to come their way. Isaac took a long pull on his captured Bud, unnoticed and alone.

He needed to pee, to empty out his day. He crossed the fir-stripped floor and ducked through a narrow door into the men's room. Inside, the ceiling was notched by the bottoms of the steps that led to rooms above the bar. The wooden steps creaked overhead, a woman's giggle confirming his suspicion. He peed, zipped his pants, then stepped back into the barroom, physical relief quickly replaced by familiar apprehension.

"Ain'tchu Isaac Moses? You were great, 32 points one game, against Lapwai, too." The grinning white face appeared above a corner of the Coca-Cola sign as the second man from the now empty booths brushed past on his way to the restroom. "Your buddy's gone to pussy heaven. He won't be down for quite awhile. Slim and me are headed back to Kamiah if you want a ride."

For a moment Isaac grasped for the strength to flee this invitation or hide in the corners of this once more unraveling day, but he jumped instead to the cheers of the crowd, arced the shot from outside the key, saw the swish of the net as his feet touched the court, heard the buzzer signal the end of the game. Certainly a hero deserved the hand on the back that turned him toward the barroom door and guided him to the Chevy pickup parked in the alley beside the brick wall that rose to a single light in an upstairs room. The light flicked off as Isaac hunched through the pick-up door, slid across the duct-taped seat and scrunched his left leg against the plastic knob on the end of the gearshift. The cold engine bucked through a grocery store parking lot, then pulled them north along Main toward the river. Slim, the driver, alternately rubbed the inside of the windshield with the heel of his hand and poked his head out the window for glimpses of the road as the heater groaned in its bearings and spilled cold air into the cab. The defroster had breathed a small clear arc at the bottom of the windshield by the time they reached the north end of the bridge. The left front brake grabbed slightly as Slim slowed for a stop sign. Then he laughed, and the pick-up swerved right onto U.S. 12 and curved unsteadily into the right hand lane, Kamiah at their back.

Isaac glanced at the driver's face in the dim light of the dashboard, laughter lines now gone, a slight twitch creeping along the stubbled jaw. Isaac's shoulders tightened, his breathing quickened.

"Hey, Isaac, relax." The man on Isaac's right slid toward the passenger door to give Isaac more room. "We're just going to make a little stop at Betty's on our way home. There's a new Injun gal up from New Mexico, just right for you. We'll all have a little fun and then head back to Kamiah. And guess what, buddy, you're buyin'."

The driver gunned the engine on the short straightaway above Scott's Grove, braked for the curve that everyone knew as Maggie's Bend, then bounced the pickup into the narrow strip of gravel that served as a parking lot. A single yellow light bulb at the end of a curved metal arm above a wooden signboard titled this jumble of well-weathered boards assembled beside the riverbank *Betty's Steambath.*

Isaac's brain began to swirl as the three men emptied the cab, alcohol and adrenaline competing for possession as he tried to size up the two men and the cold and the money in his boots and the short distance to the brown-skinned warmth beyond the golden lamplight.

Five steps from the entrance door, Slim leading, his partner by Isaac's side, Isaac made his decision. The money was his, ninety years past due. He stopped, thought of running, stood his ground.

"C'mon, Isaac. You'll like this as much as we will." The man on his left reached for his arm. Slim turned, his eyes narrowing in the light from the bulb overhead, and he landed his right fist just below Isaac's ribs. Beer and puke shot out of Isaac's mouth, spattering the face before him. He tried desperately to fill his chest with air, to run or walk or even stand. He staggered along the outside of the building, cedar siding slivering his left hand.

"You son-of-a-bitch!" was followed by "Aah, let him go."

Slim moved quickly to a pine limb lying on the gravel, a windstorm blowdown turned gnarled club. He swung, and Isaac felt his right knee buckle as he lurched toward the river's edge. The sound of rolling stones turned his head in a backward glance, and the piece of Ponderosa smashed into his right cheek. The shock of icy water fought the blackness spreading through his brain. His head lolled in a thin pool of blood lapping the side of his face as the river's current carried him away.

When his dangling right leg bounced on gravel, Isaac lifted his head to scream, but instead gulped air like a ravenous wolf. The river slowed, and his left leg searched for the bottom of the eddy that was sweeping him toward shore. He dragged himself onto a pebble beach and leaned against a driftwood log.

A growing panic spread across his chest, punctuated by the pain in his face and the odd angle of his right knee. He tried to think while he wrung what water he could from his wool jacket. He'd have to risk the bridge at the east end of town, he decided, then follow shadows to the Kooskia Inn and hope that Jimmy had lingered in Luella's bed.

He crossed the bridge with a broken stride, right knee jolting him with each step. The roadside path through East Kooskia was dark and safe, porch lights out, bar traffic gone. A dog barked at his limp as he rounded the corner near Cory's Mill, then skirted the millpond toward the center of town. From the corner of B and Main he could see the dim north wall of the Kooskia Inn, parking lot empty, Main Street still.

He began to shake. Only his right cheek was warm, and when he touched it with his fingers, blood dripped into his palm and dribbled down his wrist. A narrow set of headlights beamed up Main, a Willys with a hound box in the bed. Isaac remained in shadow, thought of his own pickup waiting for him in Kamiah, the money in his sloshy boots, the pawn stubs' ink blurring in his wet wallet. He crossed the Southfork bridge, muscles tight with cold, his right leg reluctantly joining the pace. A short walk through a pole yard brought him to the railroad tracks, a single pathway home. Behind a thin layer of scudding clouds, the moon cast its glow as through a shroud. Light snow began to fall as he found a familiar rhythm in the creosoted timbers wedged into the gravel ballast like stitches trying to hold the open wound of this night together.

For two miles he slogged along following the snow-white edges of the black-tarred ties whose path curved around the gentle bends of the river. By the end of the third mile his rhythm slowed and his right boot began to push lengthening strips of snow in front of each footprint. When he paused, he began to shake. He rubbed his hands together trying to get them warm. His skin felt numb and waxy, and he stuffed them back into the soggy pockets of his jacket. An owl hooted nearby. Isaac shook snow from his head and started again as three whitetails slipped across the tracks in front of him like phantoms.

The snow stopped falling at mile four, and pricks of starlight dimly outlined pines and serviceberry bushes beside the tracks, then a fencepost wrapped in broken wire. Muscles stiff, breathing curbed, he tried to move at a faster pace, to warm himself with motion.

Midway into the next-to-last bend of the river before the lights of Kamiah would mark his place with certainty, would beckon his way with hope, he missed a tie and stumbled. He tried to lift his arms, to hold back the earth rising quickly towards him, but his right cheek hit the cold steel rail and fresh blood broke the crusted surface of his face. He rolled onto his back between the rails, tried unsuccessfully to focus on the clearing sky, then closed his eyes. The air was dead calm, the silence soft and inviting. When he rolled onto his left side and tried to curl his legs up toward his chest, searing heat shot up his right leg. He shook his head, crawled five feet, planted his left foot and stood. A set of animal tracks pocked the snow in front of him, soft-edge fresh, a coyote headed west. Hands in pockets, Isaac followed.

At two hundred yards, the tracks disappeared, virgin snow filling the path between the rails like empty lines in a journal. At first Isaac failed to recognize the blankness of that space, his boots plowing out an entry beyond the finer print of the coyote's feet. Movement drew his eyes to the edge of the bank between the rails and the river. There the coyote paused, glanced back, then dropped out of sight. To the west the lights of Kamiah filled the bottom of the valley with a distant glow. Isaac turned, lifted his right foot awkwardly over the snow-covered rail and pursued the paw prints before him.

The coyote's trail led straight to the river's edge near a shoal that stretched downstream from the point of a wooded island. Isaac knew the crossing, the slough on the other side, the washed out hoof prints of two thousand horses herded across the river by Nez Perce boys as soldiers topped the southern rim of the valley seventy-five years before. From the gravel point mid-stream, the coyote watched Isaac stop where rhyme ice outlined the shore, then lifted its tail and waded into the quiet water. Isaac stepped into the boot-top current, following the coyotes invisible trail.

Fresh paw prints marked a cut in the far side bank at the site of the ancient crossing. When Isaac tried to ascend the bank, his boots slid on wet cottonwood leaves and he landed in a stiff pile on the rocky shore. His arms began to shake, his clenched fists unaware of their banging together on the stiff front of his frozen coat. Leaves now dislodged, a second try found traction in the sandy soil.

Near the head of a brushy draw a metal shaft from a single-carriage sawmill leaned against a pile of hewn timbers, a bearing rusted onto one end, but he could no longer place himself on a mental map. He was drowning in drowsiness. Even his shaking had stopped by the time he backed against a nearby pine, slid slowly down its craggy bark and sat, chin on chest, legs lost somewhere in front of him.

He had started to doze when he heard a faint tone, almost flat, then a soft buzz that lifted into a curve, then two, then separate notes bowing to each other, pausing, marching, climbing, dancing. The music grew louder, until the chords of a cabinet organ filled the silent void around him, pipes and bellows magnifying the movement of the polished keys in polished wood on a polished floor. He opened his eyes, tried to move his legs, rolled onto his left knee and pulled himself upright against the pine. The sound was coming from the missionary house with the split rail fence spilling shadows on the moonlit snow. The coyote walked beside the fence, then vanished.

The music grew softer as Isaac approached the abandoned house. Two fence rails had rotted at their ends, forming an unintended gate. Broken steps led to a wooden door ajar. Inside, a crack of moonlight lit whitewashed walls with circular saw cuts on the unplaned boards that finished the interior. The music stopped when Isaac pushed the door open and passed into the broadening band of light that filled the empty room. To his left, a doorway led into the second room of the house. The header brushed his stiff hair as he stepped through the opening.

A frayed blanket covered the window on the south wall. Isaac stumbled across the floor, gripped the blanket's edge between his wrists and twisted his body toward the center of the room. He heard the blanket tear and smelled the musty wool. Light flooded the room, highlighting the river stone that marched up part of the west wall, the fireplace chimney narrowing as the stones approached the ceiling. A worn mattress lay in front of a broad hearth, a tattered quilt and crumpled bedspread at its side. Between mattress and hearth a chamber pot rested lidless on the dusty floor, its porcelain edge rimmed with soot. A hardware candle stood in its center, a box of kitchen matches nearby.

With his second step toward the mattress, Isaac tripped on the blanket he was dragging, landed on his battered knee and screamed. He rolled to the matches, sat up, gripped the box between both fists and bit a corner of the cardboard sleeve. With a push of his arms and jerk of his head, the box flew open and matches spewed across the floor. He tried to pick one up, but his thumb and fingers refused to move. His eyelids drooped and closed, his body swayed, his face hit the mattress edge, and he began to float like a heavy log on a quiet stream. The yap of a coyote startled him with its closeness, and when he opened his eyes the red heads and white tips of the matchsticks teased him in the moonlight. He sat up once more, and again his right thumb and index finger refused his command. Wool blanket in tow, he rolled his left side onto the mattress, then winced as his right leg followed. He clubbed the quilt and bedspread over his feet and legs.

The moon passed beyond the last cloud chasing the brief storm east, casting light again onto the white-washed walls of this lovers' nest in the missionary house where Sue McBeth had plotted against the heathens, General Howard had prayed for victory, the Measuring Woman had carved up the land, and a small boy had held his mother's hand and listened to Bach as outside his father coughed fresh blood onto his starched white shirt.

Isaac gripped the wool blanket between his fists and slowly lifted its musty smell above his waist, onto his shoulders, over his head. He shuddered once, then slept.

CHAPTER NINE

1877

Speaks-in-Tongues sat on matted grass inside her elk skin lodge pitched on the edge of a meadow. Nipples still wet, she watched her sleeping infant son as she passed a twisted strand of Indian hemp between the fingers of her left hand, stopping at the knots and beads and shells that formed the journal of her life. Her arms ached from peeling slender lodgepole pine that grew in thickets on nearby slopes. The camp was quiet, fires low inside the eighty-two lodges pitched beside the Bitterroot River. More than two thousand horses grazed on bunchgrass along the east side of the valley. Tomorrow the people would travel leisurely up the East Fork trail, cross the divide, then camp in open country. For two months they had been fighting and fleeing soldiers—at White Bird and Camas Prairie and Cottonwood Creek. They had crossed the mountains on *Ishana Ishkit*, the trail to the buffalo, food and possessions dwindling each day. The 200 cavalrymen and 400 foot soldiers pursuing them were now far in the rear, axmen chopping the downfalls that littered the trail.

Mixing old friendships with new-found fears, the ranchers and townsfolk in the Bitterroot Valley had nervously accepted the Indians' promise of a peaceful passage, had sold them beans and bacon and sacks of flour, had even offered bullets for twice the normal price. The Nez Perces had slowed their pace, believing their unwanted war was now behind them, safety and buffalo ahead.

The latest knot in Speaks-in-Tongues' story string enclosed a granite pebble from the creek that meandered down the Lapwai Valley past the Christian mission that had molded her life. The pebble represented her baby boy, smooth and round and strong. Her older son had also been knotted into memory, and her daughter Swan Feather, whose quiet breathing stirred the hollow hair of an elk skin cover at the far side of the tipi. Speaks-in-Tongues' marriage, her grandmother's passing, her vigil on the mountain—all had been captured in fiber. The first knot had been a sad one, representing Speaks-in-Tongue's separation from her childhood friend and the beginning of betrayal. She had thought once of cutting that end of the string away, of angrily throwing it into a fire or launching it downstream in a spring torrent, but it held love as well as pain and a lesson she would never forget.

A few months before Speaks-in-Tongues was born, the Reverend and Mrs. Spalding had arrived on Lapwai

Creek, Henry stern like the white man's god, Eliza smiling like the Virgin Mary. The people had built them a lodge, brought them camas, cous, berries and fish. Liza, the missionaries' first child, arrived the following winter. Over the next few years she and Speaks-in-Tongues became like twins, bound by a language only the two of them could fully understand, English and Nez Perce words intertwined like wild clematis in a clump of ninebark. They played together in the mission house, churned cream yellow in the buttery, carded wool sheared from the flock of sheep that neatly trimmed the mission grounds. Together they learned to sew flannel dresses, to knit warm leggings, to read the *Book of Matthew* in the words of both their mothers. The two girls played at preaching in the Nez Perce tongue to children standing on the shady side of the schoolhouse. With mothers and headmen, they crowded into the school's single room with 12-pane windows and a woodstove to listen to the white man's spirit talk. Bound by an historical moment, the two girls were inseparable.

Speaks-in-Tongues was ten when Liza left for the Whitman's mission at Wailatpu, her father's stare sufficient to quell the child's protests at leaving her mother, her home, her friend. She needed to be with white children, Liza's mother had told her, for reasons Liza would not understand. Liza promised Speaks-in-Tongues she would return when the balsamroot bloomed on the hillsides north of the river. She pledged she and Speaks-in-Tongues would be friends forever.

The high-pitched calls of coyotes from the ridge above the encampment interrupted Speaks-in-Tongues' reflections. The staccato yips of pups in training followed. She shifted her fingers to the beginning of her story string and felt the human hair woven into the hemp. She recalled with sadness the news of the murders at Wailatpu and young men from her village looting the mission house at Lapwai—breaking windows, burning furniture, driving off livestock. Believing her friend Liza dead, Speaks-in-Tongues had slashed her left arm with a shard of glass from the schoolhouse window. She saw again the blood that had dripped off her fingertips into the millrace, had trickled down her back as she hacked at her waist-long hair, leaving a ragged edge above the calico collar of her white man's dress. The next day she gathered hemp along the creek, separated fiber from pith and bark, retrieved strands of her own hair and began recording the wrap and twist of her life. She later learned that Liza had survived the killings, but no balsamroot blossoms ever witnessed her return.

The braided hair of Speaks-in-Tongues older son swayed before her as he dipped his head through the entrance to the lodge. In his fourteenth year, Medicine Dog was hard as yew wood and the fastest runner among the older boys who trailed the herd each day. He had his father's walk, a springing motion as if striding on damp moss. His eyes were his mother's, so dark they shined like a freshly cleaved obsidian chip. He gave her his usual serious nod accompanied by a slight lift of his eyebrows that told her she was loved, the horses were safe, and his work was done.

When Medicine Dog spoke, Speaks-in-Tongues learned that her husband had taken the back trail with two other warriors to make certain the soldiers were still far behind. Two Crows would return at dawn, her son advised, and would sing his morning song with his son at the edge of the horse herd as each began the duties of his day.

Outside her lodge, Speaks-in-Tongues stretched toward a hint of moon. She had years earlier claimed late evening for herself, breezes breathing softly downslope, her children wrapped close to the earth. She drank from a nearby spring, then gathered dry willow for the morning fire. A new knot for her story string began to form in her mind, an ugly knot that would represent their tortured trail of the past two months—the fighting at White Bird Creek, dangerous river crossings, the roar of the cannons from the bluffs above Red Owl's village. The finest details were the clearest: black paint on brown skin, sweat and gunpowder smeared across her husband's cheek, her own body's tension damming her milk, Swan Feather's eyes as she lifted her baby brother to their mother's waiting arms as shrapnel shredded their lodge. She knew this sorry summer needed to end, that the stains on the earth should be washed with fall rain and covered with an early snow.

Back in her lodge, Speaks-in-Tongues listened to her children's breathing while she coiled her story string for its return to her favorite cedar root bag. Her fingers stopped again at the first knot in the string's two-foot length. Many winters lay between that knot and the second. Separating them was the part of her life she called the in-between, when her Christian songs and prayers became lost in the tribal anger that had ripped out the mission's millrace so Lapwai Creek could return to its bed, that had burned the mission's fences that divided the land. During this time Speaks-in-Tongues had become invisible, to her people as well as to herself.

When she was first a woman, her mother sent her to be with her grandmother, Two Stars, who could dance with the past and see dawn from the middle of the night. There Speaks-in-Tongues watched seasons of herbs, days of salves, dawns of prayer and song both anchored to the earth and floating to the sky. People came to Two Stars with gifts and left with hope, while Speaks-in-Tongues watched from the silent shadows of her life. Then Speaks-in-Tongues came together as her people split apart, one people into two and two persons into one with a new heart and a clear voice.

Henry Spalding had heralded the end of her malaise. His return to the Lapwai brought smiles from some of her people and frowns from others, canceling each other into caution. The Lapwai Valley was filling with soldiers and talk of a new treaty law. Spalding arrived in teachers' clothing, but the voice of the preacher remained. Eager to learn of Liza, Speaks-in-Tongues had walked to the agency building the day of his arrival and stood on the covered porch. She heard the soft growl of Spalding's voice inside and waited.

Mid-morning the door latch clicked and the tall but slightly stooped reverend stepped onto the porch. His bold eyes caught Speaks-in-Tongues' own before she could glance away. He spoke to her in Nez Perce, his voice demanding an answer.

Yes, she was of the Big Thunder band, she had replied. Yes, she could take a message to the village. Yes, she would tell her chief that Reverend Spalding wished to speak with him. Then Spalding turned toward the door and disappeared. That evening she found her story string with its shorn hair twisted into the nearly forgotten fiber. She knew a knot was forming. Her fingers awaited its shape, her heart awaited its meaning.

That fall more soldiers came to the Lapwai, and when the camas bloomed the following spring, three commissioners sent by Washington called the people together for a council. Chief Lawyer's band was first to arrive at the council grounds on the banks of Lapwai Creek. Soon more bands drifted into place, led by Chiefs Eagle-of-the-Light, Joseph, Red Owl and others until 3000 Nez Perces had gathered. *No*, Washington had not yet paid for the land the Nez Perces had sold them in 1855, just eight years ago, admitted commissioners Hale, Hutchins and Howe. *No*, the Americans had not kept 10,000 miners off the Indians' land. *No*, the government had not punished white men for stealing Indian horses and cattle, from peddling whiskey, from mistreating Nez Perce women. But Washington's intentions were good, the three white men declared, and the best way to solve these problems was for the Indians to sell the white man more land.

The chiefs who objected to the treaty proposal were bad men, the commissioners proclaimed, disloyal to the interests of their people. Speaks-in-Tongues remembered their words like passages she had memorized years before from the *Book of Matthew*, haunting voices she could not dispel. "When the new arrangement is made, the good Nez Perces will be wise and rich and happy," the commissioners had told the chiefs who spoke against a new treaty. "You bad Indians will be poor and miserable, and you will make your children poor and miserable. They will see that you have caused this, and when you are dead, they will curse you, because you did not secure these things to make them happy, as the wise chiefs did for their children. If you persist in your disloyalty, we shall not regard you as Nez Perces, for the white men think that to be a Nez Perce means that you are good men."

Frequently passing back and forth between the agency and the treaty grounds were the go-betweens, Henry Spalding with his Christian following, former mountain man Robert Newell with his Indian relatives, and the young Nez Perce woman whom government officials began to call "the messenger." She was always nearby. She was always willing to carry words to various factions among the bands as long as they were provided in her native tongue, the only language the officials thought she understood. Speaks-in-Tongues had been that messenger, had translated for her people all she had overheard of agency talk, of commissioner comments, of the recommendations of the other go-betweens. Spalding foresaw the confinement of the Nez Perces to a small area as helpful to his preaching. Longtime tribal friend Doc Newell had been paid for months to provide information to the commissioners. Gold on ceded land would repay treaty costs 50 times over, the Commissioners agreed, and the rich ground gained for farming would be a bonus. For Speaks-in-Tongues, each new thread of information stitched the story together and connected the fragments of her life.

On the third night of the council the leaders of all the bands met. They talked through the night about the first white men who had visited their country, led by Daytime Smoker and Grizzly Robe Folded, and of the promises made at the treaty council on Camearp Creek years before the traders and trappers arrived. They spoke of the spirit talkers and gold miners and the Walla Walla treaty and the white man's war over the black man. Some chiefs counseled war, some peace, some spoke of trust and others disdain. Just before a cloudless dawn, Speaks-in-Tongues addressed them. "It is a trick," she told them. "The commissioners lie, our friends are spies, and we are betrayed."

Two lines formed outside the longhouse as the morning star faded from view. Facing one another, chiefs and subchiefs in each line shook hands across the chasm that now separated the Nez Perce people—treaty and non-treaty, fenced and free.

That day Speaks-in-Tongues knotted a serviceberry seed into her story string as the promise of a new beginning.

An owl hooted softly over the camp pitched on the Bitterroot. Swan Feather stirred. Her baby brother's breathing was as soft as the lynx hide on which he slept. Soon, Speaks-in-Tongues decided, she would mark this time in her life with a new knot representing her people's fight and flight for freedom that her grandchildren must never forget. She would make the knot the next evening, she decided, when the people would camp, sing and dance in celebration at a place they called the Big Hole.

CHAPTER TEN

1952

Isaac stirred as the bloodstained bedspread was lifted from the right side of his face. He thought he heard a voice, and when he turned toward the sound and half-opened his left eye, a blur of red and black squares hovered above him. The odor of damp wool and cigarette smoke hung nearby. A voice said "Jesus!" and then the image was gone. He closed his eye and drifted in a dense fog.

Later, the voice returned, and another as well. "Just like I told ya, Doc. On my way to the mallard slough when I run across his tracks. Blood frozen in 'em. Led right to the cabin. Is he gonna live?"

Isaac felt fingers on the side of his neck, then a hand traveling down his side, along his right thigh to his knee, then up to his wrist. The hand stopped, measured the slow drumming rhythm where bone and flesh and blood intertwined.

“We’ve got to get him warmed up,” came a calm voice connected to that strong hand. “Let’s roll him onto this blanket. I think the two of us can carry him to the car.”

Isaac tried to turn, to roll, but his muscles refused his wish. He felt himself lifted, heard grunted admonitions, winced when his back scraped the steps at the front of the house. Twice the men set him down on the frozen ground while each sucked air from the morning.

“Those coyote tracks caught my attention too, Doc. The critter circled the cabin several times. Probably could smell the blood and followed him here.”

“Maybe,” the other man replied as they resumed half-carrying, half dragging Isaac along the short trail to the highway. At roadside, the two lifted him to a half-standing position, then slowly bent him into the back seat of Doc Ryan’s Buick. “You sit back there with him. Keep him propped up. Use your hat if he vomits.”

They crossed the bridge into Kamiah, then added car tracks to those already marking the two inches of snow covering Main. Doc u-turned at the intersection by the bank. Half a block north the Buick pushed against the curb and stopped.

“Isaac, we need to get you inside the clinic. Can you hear me, Isaac?”

Isaac nodded, tried unsuccessfully to lift himself from the car seat, raised one hand in a gesture of help. The two men soon had him sandwiched between them and the trio moved sideways through the clinic’s front door, then a second door into a side room cramped with an exam table, two chairs and a cot stuffed against the far wall. They struggled to get Isaac onto the exam table, arms and legs like frozen wood. "Turn the oil stove up, Jack, and throw that blanket on it. Then help me get him out of these damned wet clothes," Doc directed.

Boots came off first, leaving one wet sock in place and a twenty dollar bill plastered against the inside of Isaac's bare arch. Doc peeled the bill away and dropped it into a boot. The remaining sock followed, and soon more clothing lay scattered on the linoleum floor. Tepid water came next, a bowl for each hand, pain and pleasure twisted together like good hemp rope. But the Pendleton blanket was what Isaac would remember, tucked around his legs and feet with the softness of a lover in that brief time of skin on skin between passion spent and the loneliness that followed. A muffled "thanks" was the only word Isaac spoke as he settled into safety and welcomed sleep.

When Isaac awoke, his hands ached, and Doc Ryan was preparing to numb the right side of his face before sewing up the torn flesh. "You just might lose a couple of those fingers," Doc advised as they both looked at Isaac's swollen hands, his fingers turning waxy black. "And they're going to hurt a lot more than this stitching job."

"My knee?" Isaac asked.

"It's not broken, but you'll probably wish it was. Lots of stuff torn up in there. You'll be on crutches for quite awhile. So you're beat up, but alive. Could have been worse."

Seeing his patient glance around the exam room, Doc continued, "Peggy took your clothes to the laundry.

Your boots are out by the oil stove. Everything is there. Well, almost everything."

Isaac flinched as the curve of the suturing needle climbed higher on his cheekbone.

"Sorry about that," Doc said quietly as he tied off a stitch. "I gave a twenty to Jack, he's the one who found you. Asked him to buy you some groceries. You kept mumbling that you wanted to go home. He's rustling some wood, too, said he'd get a good fire going in that cabin of yours."

When the stitching was completed, Doc Ryan's assistant arrived with a bowl of oatmeal. Peggy's pleasant scent accompanied each spoonful while Isaac's aching hands rested on the blanket draped over his lap and legs. He had stretched back on the examination table, hands and face reminding him that he was indeed alive, when Jack returned, announced that the cabin was warming, and laid $7.40 on a nearby chair. Isaac tried to think of something to say, but his mind was already nestling into the softness of the pillow Peggy had placed beneath his head. "Jack," he said, then disappeared into a heavy sleep.

Late afternoon the three men struggled up the sled-tracked draw to Isaac's house. A stack of wood, dried and quartered, filled one end of the porch. An apple box of pitch sticks sat nearby. Cozy warmth had tucked itself into every corner of the house and nestled against the ceiling. Cans of all descriptions lined the back of the kitchen counter—Green Giant corn and Dole fruit cocktail and Dinty Moore stew staring out from the pile. "Eggs and bacon in your window box," said Jack as he stoked the wood stove and put coffee on to boil. Doc recommended tea instead, and then the door latch clicked and the two men were gone. With two unbandaged fingers Isaac pulled the coffee pot to the edge of the wood stove, then hobbled the short distance to his bed.

For the next several days various visitors slipped through his cabin door and sat on the bentwood chair by the wood stove. Some came with the midday sun, some came at night. Some spoke softly, some only stared, one danced. They separated his trips to the woodpile and outhouse, his fumbling efforts to open cans with his bandaged hands, his measurement of snowfalls by peeing off the end of the porch.

"Hey, you like that wood, huh? I'll bring some more in a few days, got some good butts from the defect pile. Let me put a fresh pot on, and I'll haul away them cans. I think you're bringing me good luck, Isaac. I got a new job at the mill, gonna be a saw filer now. The ol' lady is real happy." The clank of empty tin in a grocery sack followed the plaid jacket through the cabin door.

"I walked over to see you, and it's cold out there. Had a little trouble with my pickup. Tie rod bent, and a limb went through the radiator, but I'll get it fixed. I could get you a bottle if you want one, or some Bud. You still got money? I loaned some out, and it ain't comin' back very fast. I put some elk steak in your sink. It won't last long in this goddamned heat."

Isaac tried to greet his visitors with a smile, but he seldom spoke. The more they talked the less real they seemed, and he sometimes wondered if they had been there at all. Occasionally, half asleep, he would hear the woodstove door squeak, and once he found a box on the kitchen table with root cellar carrots and winter pears, a freshly-butchered chicken and a box of Lipton tea.

On the fifth day an owl and a raven sauntered in when the stove got too hot, the cabin door ajar a crack to cool the place down. In brilliant white plumage speckled with black, the owl perched on the arched back of the cabin's lone chair and stared at Isaac with eyes the color of September moons. The shiny raven squawked and cawed while dancing circles on the puncheon floor, stopped to preen a wing feather into place, then bobbed its head with another round of steps and chortles. Isaac felt a chill when both birds left, and he closed the door.

The old woman came twice. She was dressed in clay-cleansed buckskin from neck to knees, a row of elk ivories above each breast. Blue beads encircled her throat. She glided about the main room quietly observing the chinked cracks in the walls, the south window view, a pestle leaning against the sheet of asbestos behind the stove. On her second visit she carried a bundle of nettles as thick as her arm. She smiled at Isaac lying flat on his back, right leg bent over a tightly rolled blanket, a candle burning on the apple box nightstand beside him.

Isaac was sitting on the bench at the kitchen table when Doc Ryan knocked at the door, tripped the latch and poked his brown felt hat and mustached face inside. "Hello, Isaac. Thought I'd come by and take another look. Maybe even join you for a cup of tea." He set his black bag on the table, lit the burner under the teapot, straddled the paint-chipped chair and scooted in Isaac's direction.

"You're going to have a ragged scar on your right cheek here, but it's healing fine. Cheekbone was cracked but not busted. Now let's see those hands."

Isaac had removed the bandage from his right hand two days earlier, unwinding the tape with his teeth. Most of the fluid in the blisters at the tips of his fingers had been absorbed into the five rounds of fat blue flesh that poked out from his palm. Doc removed the bandage on Isaac's left hand, eyed the blackened fingertips, replaced the cotton pads between each pair of fingers and wrapped fresh gauze from fingertip to wrist. "It's time to start exercising that knee, Isaac, not a lot of weight at first, but moving it, bending it, short walks will do. Your hands will be extra sensitive to the cold, keep them covered when you go out. And now let's have that tea."

Isaac asked Doc what day it was, how the Kubs were doing, if there were many ducks on the river. He heard the man's wedding ring clink against the side of the broken-handled mug Doc was using for a tea cup and guessed from Doc's lingering sip that more advice was on its way.

Doc leaned into the space between them. "I can't really fix you, Isaac. I'd like to, just like I'd love to watch you coming down court again, taking the pass at the post, jamming the ball through the net. I do blood and bones and babies, get lucky now and then with a germ or two, but you need someone besides me." He shifted his weight on the bentwood chair. Isaac stared at his right leg and tried to make it bend.

"Do you know Raven Eye?" Doc asked after two more sips of tea.

"The old man on the Southfork?" Isaac asked.

"Yes, end of the road, that's the one. I think he would like to see you."

Isaac acknowledged the suggestion with a nod of his head, then focused once more on his aching knee.

"Heat is probably the best thing for that knee, Isaac. Go see Raven Eye and he'll fix you up. Stay warm, and thanks for the tea." Doc Ryan stood, stretched, and closed his bag. The door latch clicked as Isaac moved his right knee closer to the woodstove.

A two-day chinook wind finally coaxed Isaac out of the hollow void of his ragged healing. The blisters on the ends of his fingers were almost gone, along with an extra-large bottle of aspirin. With the warmer weather he took short walks, sometimes with one crutch, sometimes with none, throwing his right leg forward in a small arc in the melting snow. The warmer weather was a temporary respite, he knew, a chance to gather scraps of wood and a few moments of hope before icy fog and arctic air once more gripped the valley.

He also knew the time had come to cross the bridge to town. He had counted his boot money over and over, five 50s, eight 20s, and $7.60 in change. He found two more 50s wadded in the inside pocket of his jacket. He wondered whether his damaged leg would bend enough to fit into his waiting Ford, to pump the pedal three times for a faithful start, to coax the truck to speed. Moving his foot to the brake pedal worried him the most, left leg punched to the floor, right knee trying to bend beneath the wheel, pick-up sliding through the rarity of a stop sign or into the frequency of a ditch. But the ledger book was troubling him most. Not the book by his bed with its neatly penciled columns, but his mother's Carlisle ledger book with sorrow captured on every page. The "Closed till Tuesday" notice taped to the pawnshop door had become anchored in the middle of his mind, along with the pawn ticket retrieved from his wet wallet with November 18, 1952 blurred across its surface. This was the scene where he stumbled, where he couldn't find his lines. The threads to his past were growing thinner and fewer, his future untethered, adrift. But his immediate needs were wood and meat, hence chainsaw, rifle and pickup.

The creek by the side of his cabin ran flush with melt when Isaac stuffed his money into his jeans pocket, parked his crutches on the porch and limped toward the river. An unexpected stream of pickups followed the river road toward town, a shift-change number of rigs that didn't belong there in the middle of the day. He heard an engine slow, then Jack Smith's gravelly voice. "Headed to town, Isaac? I'll take yuh over, save that leg a bit."

"What's goin' on?" Isaac asked as he pulled his stiff leg carefully into the cab.

"It's the shits, Isaac. A goddamned shutdown. Lumber market's gone to hell. Half the day shift furloughed this week, the rest gone by Tuesday. Maybe a month. Probably more. Wild game will sure catch hell. We'll all be Indians this winter."

They crossed the bridge in silence, predators of different packs each wondering what to say. Jack broke the silence. "Are you headed to Doc Ryan's? I can drop you off at Main Street."

"I'm gonna get my pickup, need to get some wood in. It's at Texaco, but anywhere here is fine. And Jack, thanks for everything."

Jack glided his Chevy to a roadside stop, and Isaac opened the door and slid both legs over the end of the seat. "Be careful in the bars," added Jack as Isaac's left foot caught ground and cushioned his move. "It'll be a rough winter for us all."

Isaac crossed to the west side of Main, limped south past the grocery and butcher shop, the post office and jewelry store. Easy smiles and holiday spirit made it apparent the news hadn't yet hit town.

Nick Snodderly had heard of the shutdown by the time Isaac breached the front door of the Texaco Station, Christmas bells on the doorknob announcing his entrance. Nick had just put down the phone, it's scratched black surface smudged with grease, and the creases of his face refused the slightest bend as he greeted Isaac bluntly. "Thought I'd see you pretty soon. That battery was no good, sat out there too long dead. You didn't pay much for it anyway. I can sell you a two-year one for fourteen bucks. That's new, with exchange, green stamps if you like."

Isaac fingered his cash, made his decision, and moved to his script. "I came for my rifle. You weren't here when I paid for the truck. Paid cash for it all, but the kid didn't know where my rifle was. Said you must have it somewhere."

"I didn't want to leave it here." His voice softened, his shoulders slumped. "That's a valuable gun. It's your gun. I'll bring it in tomorrow."

“Good, and I’ll take the battery. I’ve got the money on me. You can put a quick charge on it and stick it in the truck. I’ll be back in an hour.”

The hardware store was easy, two Lincolns and a Jefferson melting tension like a third beer on a Saturday night. “Not everybody’s paying,” the store owner told Isaac in a serious tone, leaving little doubt as to who was being referred to and suggesting that Isaac was at least partially responsible for such collective malfeasance. Isaac put the ten in change from paying his bill in his breast jacket pocket, his self-declared earnings of the day for maintaining his composure.

He was ready for fun by the time he entered the grocery store. The cart came first, leading him through the aisles, his leg in exaggerated stiffness. He dropped into the cart two pounds of bacon, a dozen eggs, oranges and a box of tea. By the time he entered the third aisle, he saw the clerk alert the store manager, who came out of his office and pretended to straighten some cereal boxes near the checkout counter. Isaac continued his gimpy stroll and dropped more items into his cart—Holsum bread and a pound of coffee, the new Oleo Margarine that turned yellow when you squeezed it—then limped to the checkout.

The manager had moved to the till, a short man of 45, as serious as he was bald, a nervous twitch in his left eye. He started speaking with “You owe us,” stopped as Isaac turned his face toward the counter, stared at the jagged rip on Isaac’s cheek. He asked in an uncertain tone, “Do you have any money for us today, Isaac?”

“Ring it all up.” Isaac responded. “I’m a rich Indian.” He broke the tension with a grin, reached into his left pants pocket and counted out five twenties.

“You must have been in a hell of a wreck,” the manager muttered at least partially to himself, then summoned the lingering clerk, took Isaac’s bill from his apron pocket and told the clerk to ring up the sale. With a terse smile he returned to his office in a plywood-cordoned corner of the store, *for sale* signs and bulletins tacked to the wood like children’s art in an elementary school.

Isaac left his groceries with the clerk, two sacks in a box, and said he’d be back in half an hour. He crossed the street to the clothing store, put a pair of two-dollar mule-hide gloves on the counter with three twenty dollar bills, then added more change to his keeper pocket along with his bill for $26.90 stamped PAID in fresh black ink.

Back on the sidewalk, a warm smile turned his head toward the opening door at Doc Ryan’s clinic. “How ya doin’, Isaac?” Peggy asked as she stepped onto the sidewalk and quickly closed the distance between them. “Doc said you were warmed up and dried out. Looks like that leg is pretty stiff yet, saw you earlier walking across the street.”

“I’m getting my truck today, that’ll get me around.” Isaac informed her, sharing a cautious grin. “Is Doc in?”

“No, he’s up at Winona. A lady had some trouble having her baby. Want me to tell him anything?”

“Tell him I haven’t forgotten his advice, heat for my leg and all.”

Peggy smiled again, wished him a Merry Christmas, and headed toward the bank. Isaac returned to the west side of Main. Nick had just started the Ford when Isaac cleared the corner of the car lot. Half-choked, the engine idled roughly, slowly warmed, then smoothed as Isaac fed it gas with a painful flex of his right foot. He drove to the pumps and crossed the rubber hose that rang the service bell inside. Nick filled his tank and added saw gas and chain oil to the tab. He had forgotten the $3.60 credit from the previous bill, but added it in when Isaac agreed to pass on the green stamps.

"I'll come by tomorrow for my rifle," Isaac reminded Nick as he put a fifty on the counter and the cash register door popped open. "Need to get some meat in before the mill workers chase all the game out of the country," he added with a grin.

By the time Isaac parked in front of the grocery store, his knee reminded him of what he had forgotten in his earlier shopping. He purchased the largest bottle of aspirin available and added it to the sack he carried to his pickup. He broke the bottle's seal and swallowed two as he walked around the rusted hood and glanced at the pawnshop. With his last two fifties, a twenty and two fives in his left jacket pocket and both pawn tickets in his right, he started across the street.

Bill Sheffield was placing a pair of beaded moccasins into a crowded display case when Isaac stepped through the pawnshop door avoiding as much limp as he could. A cornhusk bag covered papers piled on the rolltop desk that filled one end of the pawnbroker's makeshift office. With a glance Isaac's way, Sheffield circled the end of the display case, moved quickly to the metal grate that served as a door to the back room of the shop and slid the grate shut. When the pawnbroker turned back toward the display case, the two men stared at one another, each looking for a feint or flinch.

Isaac chose not to speak, his final solution to the practiced lines he had earlier abandoned. The two pawn tickets came first, placed firmly on the display case top, then covered with the appropriate cash. Sheffield studied the tickets, picked up one with a twenty and a five, then nodded his head toward a rack against the far wall. "Your chainsaw's over there. Get it and get out."

The fresh scar on Isaac's cheek began to throb. His eyes narrowed and his right hand balled. "You closed the shop. I was here at 4:15. You knew I had the money."

Sheffield shot back with cold confidence. "You could have come on Saturday. That was the 19th. That's what's on your ticket."

"Your sign said you were closed till Monday." Isaac narrowed the gap between them. Sheffield backed toward the steel bars behind him.

"I opened Saturday afternoon." The right side of the pawnbroker's upper lip curled beneath his bushy mustache.

"I couldn't walk on Saturday afternoon," Isaac spat into the air between them.

"It's not my fault you got drunk and shot off your mouth in a Kooskia bar."

Isaac's mind blurred. He took one step back from the display case, raised his left foot to kick in its glass front, but his right knee buckled, his six-three frame pirouetted awkwardly as he fell to the floor. The pawnbroker stepped quickly to the case between them and swept it's glass top with the back of his hand, money and pawn ticket falling on the floor around Isaac's crumpled form.

"At least the ledger book will end up with someone who knows its value, not a drunk Indian who will pawn it for a hundred bucks. Now get out of here or I'll call the cop."

When Isaac stood he was facing the door, and it seemed the only direction he could go. He stumbled down the concrete steps that led to the sidewalk, crossed the street, crawled into the cave of his pickup cab and shook. The engine caught with the first turn of the key and idled as he watched three men cross Fourth and disappear into the Boots and Saddles Bar. Next the door of the pawnshop opened and Sheffield set a chainsaw on the sidewalk. The OPEN sign in the window swung from view, then reappeared as CLOSED, and the shade behind it lowered like a vertical curtain on a narrow stage with an audience of one.

CHAPTER ELEVEN

1877-1878

Medicine Dog knelt by the creek that twisted north through crumbling banks, ice edging the dark water that flowed from the Bear Paw Range. Prairie grass lay brittle on nearby hills. An occasional low ridge afforded limited protection from a sharp northerly breeze. He heard the horses stir on the flat behind him as he scooped water into his cupped hands and drank. Soon he could rest, he told himself, but today he would help herd the ponies one more time. He wiped his mouth with the back of his hand and headed in their direction.

With the one-armed general and his soldiers well in the rear and Grandmother's Land only three days ahead, Chief Looking Glass had ordered a pause, a late departure, a needed rest. The camp lay quiet in the pre-dawn light.

The sudden sound of a thousand horse hooves beating the frozen ground cut Medicine Dog's stride, pulled his eyes to the horizon on his right where puffs of white smoke from the barrels of rifles splattered against a dull gray sky. He began to run. By the time the soldiers of the 2nd Cavalry had flanked the north end of camp, he was sprinting directly toward them and the Indian horse herd, the prize he knew would determine the winners and losers of the day.

The horses stirred. Medicine Dog looked for a wedge of open space, an angle through which to slice his share, willing to settle for two hundred head, then forty good mounts, next a pony to top and ride away from the melee now surrounding him. On his right he saw an Indian dashing for a narrow coulee, bullets scattering rocks beside his path. A feathered rider on a mousey gray tried to turn the herd toward camp, clutched his ribs and slid down the side of his horse. Medicine Dog caught a nervous paint and swung up onto its dusty back. He could hear the shouts of bluecoats as they raced a circle around the herd, the horses blowing, rearing, pawing the churning air. And then he saw a face through the dust, a short brown beard, a raised blue arm. He heard a sharp crack as a searing streak burned across his forehead. His left leg rubbed the coarse hair on his horse's back as he fell into the blackest day of his fourteen years.

Late that afternoon a raven found him. The glossy black bird danced on his chest and smelled the blood crusted across his forehead. Medicine Dog groaned and tried to raise an arm in protest, but with its powerful beak the raven plucked the boy's right eye from his face. With the eye in its beak, the bird hopped into the air, gained altitude and circled the battle scene. When it returned, the bird landed again on Medicine Dog's chest and set the stolen eye in the cleft of the boy's chin as Medicine Dog dangled between earth and sky. Then the raven spoke.

"I bring you a gift," the bird announced. "This eye has lost its color and will no longer see the day. You have another eye for that." The bird looked to the left and right, as if making certain no one was watching this transaction. "This eye I return to you will see tomorrow. But you must always look behind you as well, for your footprints are never your own." The bird then placed Medicine Dog's right eye back in its socket and flew away.

The boy strained to look back, to recall where he had been. He remembered bullets riddling his family's lodge at the Big Hole where fear and duty had propelled him through the willows on the riverbank toward the horse herd, screams and fire filling the dew-laden air. He recalled chasing the horses at Canyon Creek and swimming the herd across the Missouri at Cow Creek Crossing. He remembered the horses here at Snake Creek, the smell of trampled grass, a blue-coated arm pointing at him through the swirling dust.

He rolled over and began to crawl, to look for water, for a place to hide or die. When his rock-scraped hands found a sliver of creek in a narrow coulee, he lowered his face into the cold water and drank. His cheeks grew sticky as the water moistened the crusted blood on his forehead. He tried to stand, but stumbled and fell. Planted unsteadily on his knees, he smelled smoke, not the clean odor of burning fir but the musty sweetness of dried buffalo chips. Only then did he remember this narrow valley twisted like a snake across the prairie and the puffs of white smoke he'd seen at dawn on the ridgeline. He crawled a few more yards along the creek bank until his arms gave way and his chest and face settled on the trampled ground. He thought he heard his mother's voice calling his name, and then felt himself lifted, cradled, surrounded by a black sky.

"Drink this water." The voice was soft and pleading, the water cold on Medicine Dog's cracked lips. He tried to swallow, felt the water flow from the side of his mouth and down his chin. He swallowed again. The hands that held his head were thin and cold.

"It's Swan Feather. You must drink."

Medicine Dog opened his eyes. He saw his sister's face, her slender neck and narrow shoulders. The right side of his view was blank. A baby cried, and when he lifted his head he saw women and children huddled in dim light, the fog from their breathing layered in the narrow space above them.

Swan Feather felt his cheek with her palm, urged him to sit up, helped him drink again from the tin cup she held to his lips.

"They brought you here two days ago. You were covered with blood, asleep, maybe dead."

Medicine Dog forced himself to a half-sitting position, turned his head so he could see more of his surroundings. He was in a cave dug into a sandy bank. The far side of the cave was open, sunlight cut occasionally by a passerby.

"Where is our father?" Medicine Dog asked, glancing again toward his sister.

"The soldiers are everywhere," Swan Feather replied. "He is fighting."

An artillery shell burst nearby, shaking the ground. Women pulled blankets over their children's heads, muffling the sound of crying. Medicine Dog inched his way to the dugout's open side and stepped uneasily into the bright light. Swan Feather followed. When he tried to walk, the earth moved in strange directions. When he tried to think, his mind moved like the earth in a rolling, dizzy motion. When his left eye had adjusted to the light, he looked on either side of him. The camp itself was empty of men and full of confusion. Women wailed while digging pits into the sandy sides of the creek bank with pots and root-digging sticks. Children huddled by smoky fires and shivered in the cold. He heard occasional rifle fire and flinched when another artillery shell hit somewhere in the distance on his blind side.

An old man approached, laid part of a buffalo robe on the ground and motioned for Medicine Dog to join him. He offered buffalo jerky and cold tea, and the boy gladly accepted both.

"You are the son of Two Crows and Speaks-in-Tongues," he said, a statement begging an answer. Medicine Dog nodded.

"I am Daytime Smoker. My father was the red-headed chief when the soyapos first visited our land. Your grandfather Runs-Like-a-Deer and I were friends before the white spirit talkers came," he continued. "before even the trappers. Before we were your age now." He spoke calmly, like those no longer afraid to die. "I joined you on the Bitterroot," he added, "two days before the Big Hole."

Medicine Dog nodded again, remembering the old man with his wife and daughter riding the East Fork trail, believing as they all did then that the fighting with the soldiers was over.

"It is good you are alive again," Daytime Smoker told him, glancing at the scabbed furrow across the boy's forehead.

"Have you seen my father?" Medicine Dog asked. "He should know I am alive."

"Your father is on the ridge between us and the soldiers. He did not come in last night."

Medicine Dog finished the tea, began chewing on a second strip of jerked buffalo.

"I will go now," advised Daytime Smoker, his voice calm in the chaos that surrounded them. "I am glad your sister found me."

When Medicine Dog approached a wet wood fire, women stared at his face, then opened their circle so he could feel the warmth. The sounds of their voices drifted with the smoke. The old men and what chiefs remained would gather this morning, the women said. Toolhoolhootzote was dead, and Ollicot as well. Rainbow had been shot through his right shoulder. Lean Elk was dying from a bullet through his hip. The young men would once more retrieve the dead soldiers' rifles in the darkest part of the night.

The next day the number of wounded warriors in camp grew, and Medicine Dog joined them in small circles of tattered blankets marked with bullet holes and blood. Two Crows was not among them.

That afternoon Chief Thunder-Rolling-Over-the-Mountains spoke to the warriors. He had talked with the bear-coated army chief, he told them. The one-armed general would soon arrive with additional troops. More killing was sure to follow. If the Indians would give up their guns, the army chief said, they could return to Idaho. Thunder-Rolling-Over-the Mountains wanted to quit the fighting, wanted to look for their children, wanted to bury their dead. Later in council, Chief White Bird disagreed. He believed the six messengers sent to Sitting Bull in Grandmother's Land had gotten through, that Sitting Bull would soon appear with a thousand warriors eager to settle an old score. The white man and their word could not be trusted, White Bird exclaimed. He would rather die a free man. All the other chiefs were dead.

The following day, the fighting was over. Just before dark, Daytime Smoker came to Medicine Dog, his gray hair freshly brushed and braided. He laid a hand on Medicine Dog's shoulder.

"I found your father this afternoon," he stated calmly. "We will bury him at sunrise." Medicine Dog shuddered beneath the old man's touch, but made no reply.

"The soldiers have pulled their pickets," Daytime Smoker continued, "and Grandmother's Land is not far away. White Bird did not give up his rifle, and he and many of his people will leave this place by the middle of the night. You may want to join them."

"My sister," Medicine Dog began, then paused.

Daytime Smoker paused as well, then spoke reassuringly. "Swan Feather is worn thin. She should stay with the young and the old. We will travel south, and the soldiers will not kill us anymore."

The evening star glowed briefly between heavy clouds, then disappeared. "I will go," Medicine Dog stated in acknowledgement of the old man's message, the three words forged in sadness and determination.

Daytime Smoker slid his right hand beneath his blanket robe and lifted something into the smoky air. His left hand gripped the metal head of a pipe tomahawk, his right the tiger maple handle. "For your journey," he said, extending both arms toward Medicine Dog, adding, "This pipe was in your father's hand. He would want you to have it."

Medicine Dog took the pipe tomahawk, the head cold, handle smoothly worn. He nodded toward Daytime Smoker.

"I will tell White Bird you will join him," the old man said, then sidled east in the direction of White Bird's camp.

In the darkest hour of the night, Medicine Dog joined clumps of riders skirting snowdrifts on the ridgelines north of Snake Creek. They sang their mourning songs in silence, leaving behind their frozen dead, their nearly dead, the weary and the wounded, the old and the young. For the first few hours, no one spoke, hearing only the occasional snort of a horse. With the first pale light, three riders became six, then a dozen and more—small groups trickling north in desperate uncertainty.

White ground and gray sky filled Medicine Dog's days in Grandmother's Land, fresh buffalo hide tipis pushing back the prairie wind. They had survived, 35 lodges of Nez Perces exiled in a friendly but foreign land. In the mornings the people prayed, at night they danced. Medicine Dog had physically healed, a deep scar across his forehead, his right eye milky white. He was known now as Raven Eye, a young man with the gift of special vision.

At night he dreamed in color—balsamroot yellow on newly green hillsides, the deep blues of the Kooskooskee River on a cloudless day, the rich reds of chokecherries hanging in autumn haze. His dreams always ended with his riding toward the late day sun until he was home.

By the moon of the first salmon, he could think of nothing else. He imagined the first bleats of spotted fawns and the gentle coos of mourning doves. He remembered spring chinook edging river seams. A growing restlessness pushed up out of the thawing ground until his body felt like a bowstring stretched and drawn.

They left before the moon of eels, five men with guns, ten cartridges each, two old men, nine women, five children and Raven Eye. They traveled light, one horse apiece, safety behind them, home ahead.

Bluecoats tracked them on the fourth day of their journey, long knives at their sides. The small band hid in a rocky coulee, hoping to avoid a fight. One of the old men smoked a pipe, and a thick fog covered the land. They passed the soldiers unseen.

Once, they skirted a town at night, past barns and houses stretching into the sagebrush. South, the trail up Flint Creek turned wagon wide. That afternoon they came upon a white man with a red mustache standing in a muddy pool. Striped suspenders stretched across his back as he shoveled gravel into a wooden box. His rifle leaned against a tree thirty feet downstream. Two more men dug holes in the bank on the other side of the creek.

Food. That is what the warriors signed. They wanted to trade for food. The three men shouted and ran for their guns. One man raised his rifle and pointed it in the warriors' direction, so the warriors shot him. The other two miners died as well. Hungry still, the group rode on.

Two other miners gave them flour, and the warriors shook their hands. But the next day the long-knives chased them, firing through the trees. With two scouts in front and a strong rear guard, the exiles fled.

Finally, welcomed by familiar peaks, the band rode up the West Fork trail. A new urgency rode with them now, deeper than the strength of flight, pulling them through mountain passes and across snowmelt streams. On the fourth day of their mountain crossing, they arrived exhausted at a creek that knew their names. A full year had passed since the start of their journey. Cornered, they had fought; chased, they had run. Hunger and pain had filled their days, fear and hope their nights. But they had survived. The circle was complete. They were home.

The next afternoon three Nez Perce men rode into their camp—hair short, shirts white, pants black. They were agency men, their spokesman explained, policemen who would turn them in, this group of non-treaties, of warriors and bad-hearted heathens, the cause of all the trouble. A warrior whipped the lead agency man with his quirt, but the message remained: the non-treaty Nez Perces had no home. They would now be hounded and hunted in their own land.

When a bright half-moon lit a timbered ridge on the west side of the meadow where they camped, Raven Eye quietly said his goodbyes. He would rather live like a coyote, he told his friends, than be penned like a pig or cow. With his father's rifle slung by his saddle and a pipe tomahawk at his belt, he led his horse into the night.

CHAPTER TWELVE

1952

Hoar frost thick on roadside pines glistened in the morning sun as Isaac followed a familiar route. The sound of the Ford's engine enabled a steady speed, the truck at forty-five, the speedometer needle at zero. He knew where he was going but felt no urgency to arrive.

His destination was the home of a *tewat*, Raven Eye, a follower of the ancient ways that still existed in box canyons and cedar groves and in the corners of an occasional house where the scent of sweetgrass clung to faded wallpaper. Isaac took the first bridge into Kooskia, rattled down its Main Street, accelerated past the grass airstrip just south of town. Three miles later he crossed the Southfork and curved back north, the road abandoning the riverbank for a broad cobbled flat. Basalt bluffs on the east side of the valley shaded the ground between river and road. On his left the copper-capped tower of the Southfork Presbyterian Church basked in sunlight. The road ended at three buildings of descending size — a pole barn with a galvanized roof, a one-window shack with rough-sawn siding, and an outhouse leaning west. A chimney pipe poked above the roofline on the east end of the shack. A stack of lodge poles leaned against the other.

With Isaac's hesitant knock, the screen door repeatedly slapped the main door's frame. He pushed the screen door forward and tried three more knocks on solid wood. An invitation filtered through the wall, a barely audible sound that might have been imagined, but Isaac opened the door and stepped into a room with shapes dimly outlined by the light from the four panes of the small window in the south-facing wall.

An old man gradually came into view, propped against the wall opposite the door. He sat on a blanket on the wooden floor, nodded toward an empty rocker nearby, struck a kitchen match. The yellow flare revealed deep facial lines, silver hair hanging in braids on both sides of his chest, a forehead divided by a broad horizontal scar. He lowered the match to a hardware candle stuck to a saucer on the floor before him.

"I have waited for you for a very long time," the man said softly as he stared at the light of the candle.

"Do you know who I am?" Isaac inquired.

"Do you know who you are?" the old man replied.

"I'm Isaac Moses, from Kamiah."

The *tewat* sat silently for some time, then turned his face toward Isaac. "Tell me who you are."

Isaac glanced around the room. At the east end a woodstove sat between two short stacks of split red fir, thick bark still attached. An elk skin, tanned hair-on, lay folded on the floor near a hand-carved three-legged milk stool. A parfleche painted with geometric designs hung from a spike in the wall above the old man's head.

Isaac hesitated, then answered. "My mother is Mary Moses. She went to Carlisle. My father was Jimmy Girardoux. He died in the first world war."

The odor of wood smoke permeated the room. The old man sat in silence.

Isaac slid from the edge of the rocker to the puncheon floor, tucked his left leg in under him and waited. Seconds seemed like minutes, and when he could stand the silence no longer, he added, "My grandmother was Walking Woman. My grandfather was Billy Moses. My other grandmother died at Big Hole, my grandfather at Bear Paw."

The tewat shifted slightly on his blanket and stared at the glow of the candle, then finally asked, "What do you want from me?"

Isaac tried to focus on something other than the question lumped before him. He studied the old man's eyes, one black, the other milky white. When he could wait no longer, he spoke. "I don't know. Did Doc Ryan tell you I was coming?"

A pitch pocket crackled in the wood stove. The old man rocked back and forth slowly. "I have known you would come since the day I buried your father. It is good that you are here."

The rhythm of their conversation settled Isaac, and after several seconds he asked in a calm voice, "You knew my father?"

"I know your people. They are who you are looking for."

Rectangular patches of sunlight spread up the wall behind the old man and sharpened the red and yellow designs on the parfleche bag.

"Why do you think I am looking for someone?"

"Why else do you come to see a blind old man?"

Isaac matched the tewat's silence with his own and watched as Raven Eye again turned his face toward the candle flame and wrinkled his cheeks into a gentle smile.

"Did my father ever come here?" Isaac inquired.

"He liked to race the ponies," the tewat stated matter-of-factly. "Sometimes he and his friend would sweat by the river. They were young. They liked the stories."

Isaac studied the old man's face, followed his braids down his denim shirt to narrow hands resting on each bony thigh. "My father was a warrior," Isaac said firmly.

"Your father was a soldier. Have you been to Nialapuu?"

Isaac searched his memory for that word, that place, some conversational dot on a mental map of the region, but the dot kept roaming, refusing to land. "Where is Nialapuu?" he asked.

"North side, downstream from where the ancients lived at the bend of the river below the Kamiah crossing. There's a pool at the head of the canyon. Walking Woman went there sometimes."

"You knew my grandmother?"

"I have been on the river for a long time."

"Did she come here too?" Isaac asked, forgetting to maintain the deliberate pace of their conversation.

“She loved the river. It sang to her, and she listened to the stones.”

Isaac’s right knee began to ache. He stretched his leg, winced, asked, “Should I feed the fire?”

“Two small sticks.”

Isaac rose, took four long steps and put two sticks of wood on the bed of coals in the cast iron firebox. The room was warmer near the stove, and he sat on the folded elk skin and propped his right leg on top of the milk stool.

“You limp. Do you visit Old Man?”

Isaac stared once more at Raven Eye, tried to separate the voice from that wrinkled body, to understand the question as the scene he was part of flowed together and gently rubbed his brittle edges. “I saw Doc Ryan a few times. He told me to come see you.”

“Old Man is down by the river,” the tewat said in his rhythmic voice. “There’s wood in the barn, matches by the woodstove. Take the trail to the river. Build a good fire. The stones are waiting. When they are hot, come back and get me.”

Hoping these brief directions would all make sense, Isaac picked up the box of matches and moved towards the door. The smell of a snuffed candle followed him into the bright sunshine now streaming down the valley, and he squinted as he closed the door and turned onto the trail to the pole barn. Unchinked logs layered the first three feet of the structure. A series of posts supported rafters, ridgepole and hand-peeled nailing strips covered with corroded metal. Two hackamores hung on a nail inside the gateless entry near a neatly piled stack of cedar kindling and split tamarack. Isaac gathered five sticks of kindling and an armload of dry wood, then returned to the main trail along the south side of the barn. The path dropped over a shallow bank and ended at a sweat lodge near the riverbank. Isaac dropped the wood beside a firepit a few feet in front of the rawhide flap covering the entrance. Thin smoke and the smell of burning cedar soon wrapped around the naked cottonwoods nearby.

Raven Eye was dozing when Isaac returned to the house. The old man wrapped himself in his blanket, then led Isaac from house to barn, barn to sweat lodge. When they arrived, he gave final instructions about the placement of the hot rocks inside the lodge and the gathering of water from the Southfork in a cedar bucket. He removed his moccasins and placed them on a piece of canvas just outside the sweat lodge entrance. Isaac glanced up and down the riverbank as Raven Eye slid out of the rest of his clothing and backed his wiry body into the dark interior of the dome. Isaac placed his blacktopped sneakers and jersey socks on the canvas as well. Damp earth chilled the bottom of his feet as he also disrobed. Naked, he squeezed his lanky body backwards through the open flap of the sweat lodge and grimaced with the angle of his right knee this move required. He had just finished arranging himself on a cedar bark mat when the old man pulled the door flap closed.

The silence surrounding them was punctuated occasionally by the hiss of water Raven Eye dipped from the cedar bucket and sprinkled on the hot rocks. When Isaac closed his eyes he could hear the old man's breathing and the creaking of the willow framework overhead as it stretched with the heat and rubbed against its canvas cover. Finally the tewat spoke.

"Old Man once told me a story here. A rabbit lived in the willows by the river. In his first spring the grass was tender, the willow buds sweet, and the sun warmed him as he danced beside the water. Rabbit grew large and strong. One day he discovered a rabbit living in the river in a deep pool at the head of a rapid. Fearing that this water rabbit might come on land, Rabbit kicked him, and the water rabbit immediately kicked back. When Rabbit jumped away from the water's edge, the water rabbit disappeared. The next day Rabbit went looking for the water rabbit again. At the same time of day and at the same place in the river, he found water rabbit staring angrily up out of the water. Rabbit kicked him, and once more the water rabbit kicked back, and Rabbit retreated into the willows. When he found the water rabbit on the third day, Rabbit was ready for battle. The two rabbits kicked and hit and bit each other until their legs were flailing and blood was running down their soft brown fur. With a final attack, Rabbit plunged into the water, but one of his legs had been broken and he could not swim, and the current below the eddy swept him away." Raven Eye sighed and was quiet.

Isaac's eyes remained closed. He could barely hear the old man breath. His own breathing was quiet and deep. Sweat rolled down the side of his nose, along the valley above his right nostril and onto his upper lip. He tasted salt. He heard the wooden dipper again touching the side of the bucket, the hiss of steam, the intake of his own breath with the rapidly rising humidity.

After several more minutes had passed, the old man lifted the ladle and pushed it against the entrance flap. When Isaac opened his eyes, a crack of light was turning steam to mist, and through the haze the old man smiled.

"It is good that we are here." His voice circled the sweat lodge, passed over the river-worn stones and settled on Isaac with the reassurance of a blanket. "Your father sweated here, your grandmother too."

Isaac started to speak, but recognized he had nothing to say. He stretched his right leg, flexed his knee. It felt liquid and smooth.

"In the spring we'll get fresh nettles for your knee." Raven Eye grinned when he followed this announcement with a confident request. "Next time you come to steam, bring me some wood."

CHAPTER THIRTEEN

1877

Two Crows slacked his horse to a lazy gait, then stopped atop a bluff of weathered basalt jutting out of the prairie that filled a half-day's ride to the east. In moist dips of ground, blue camas painted their promise across the landscape. New grass stood tall as the belly of a horse off winter range. Mountains cleaved the sky to the south and west. East, they formed a long white line above the dark river canyons that swallowed the prairie's edge.

He watched his people trailing north below him, a stream of horse-drawn travois, colorful robes, young boys herding the extra mounts, lean dogs working the fringe. They had come from Wallowa, down the Imnaha, across the Snake and Salmon Rivers. The people had been called to council, to listen to a soldier chief, to explain once more that they had never sold their land, that this was where the Creator had placed them, that every clump of grass, tree, root and rock was part of them, individually and collectively, forever.

In earlier councils Two Crows had learned that the white man had a difficult time understanding simple truths. With the curiosity and excitement of youth, he had witnessed his people's first major council with the white strangers. Yakimas, Walla Wallas, Umatillas, Palus, Nez Perce—over three thousand Indians had paraded and danced, listened and talked. They had finally agreed that the white man could have some land. But from where Two Crows had ridden the past three days to the ridge of mountains on the eastern horizon was Nez Perce country, guaranteed forever by treaty papers signed by the headmen of the Nez Perce bands, by the head council of the white man's nation, by the great white father in Washington.

Just eight years later the white man had wanted more land. In a second council, the American commissioners had divided the Nez Perce into treaty Indians and non-treaties, Christians and Dreamers, tearing apart centuries-old bonds of the people. And now the people would meet once more with the white chiefs, would explain again that they never sold more land, that they were part of the land itself, brothers and sisters to the seeds, the fish and the stones.

Fort Lapwai lay square to the compass on a flat on the west side of Lapwai Creek, buildings facing inward—officers' quarters to the west, barracks on the east, office to the south, guard house on the north. According to U.S.

officials, the two-company army post had been built to protect the Indians from the ravages of lawless miners and illegal cattlemen trespassing on the reservation. In nine years of operation, no Indian's stolen horse had ever been recovered.

With vermilion striped across his forehead and extending into the part in his hair, Two Crows joined the parade of beads, blankets, paint and ponies that circled the fort. Riders' voices were raised in a shrill and searching sound that filled the parade grounds. Band by band they rode, painted warriors followed by women in buckskin dresses and brightly colored shawls. At the end of the third passing, all dismounted and filed silently toward a large canvas tent pitched in front of the guardhouse. Two Crows took a position to the right of Ollicot, who with his older brother Thunder-Rolling-Over-The Mountains was seated on one of the benches set up on the parade grounds for the occasion. During an opening prayer by a Christian Nez Perce, Two Crows counted the soldiers by the barracks and the guards posted near the front corners of the council tent. By prior agreement, all Indian guns had been left at their encampment on Sweetwater Creek a short distance up the valley. Two Crows reached beneath the blanket hanging loosely over his shoulders and touched the pipe tomahawk at his belt for reassurance.

At the completion of the prayer, with neither welcome nor greeting, the Indian agent announced that Washington had decided that all Indians must come on the reservation and must do so immediately. Years had passed since they had sold their lands to the government, the agent declared through his interpreter. It was now time for the non-reservation Indians to join their Christian brothers, to bring their stock and till the land provided them. A guttural groan rippled through the assemblage before the interpreter finished translating the last sentence.

Toolhoolhootzote, the broad-chested chief previously chosen by the Indians as their speaker, rose slowly to his feet. He glanced at the bow-tied Indian agent, then turned to face the one-armed general seated on the far side of a pine-slab table beneath the canopy that extended the front of the council tent. In a deep voice Toolhoolhootzote spoke of the earth as the Indians' mother, reminded the soldier chief that it was wrong to scar the earth with hoe or plow, that the earth could not be sold or given away, that the earth was part of his body and that he could never give up the earth. Two Crows joined in the murmuring *ahs* of agreement that swept through the warriors spread across the parade grounds.

As the interpreter repeated Toolhoolhootzote's message, the general's eyes narrowed. His face tightened. His lips quivered within the bristles of his black beard and mustache. The two rows of brass buttons down the front of his uniform straightened into vertical lines as he stood to confront Toolhoolhootzote, this barrier between him and the fulfillment of his orders. He began to speak, his voice wrapped in irritation.

"We do not wish to interfere with your religion, but you must talk about practicable things. Twenty times over you repeat that the earth is your mother and about chieftainship of the earth. Let us hear no more but come to business at once."

The quiet murmuring amongst the crowd on the parade grounds stopped.

"I have heard about a bargain, a trade, between some Indians and the white men concerning the land," Toolhoolhootzote continued. "But I belong to the land out of which I came."

Following the interpreter's translation, General Howard's response was immediate. "The Nez Perces did make such an agreement. Since the non-treaty Indians were in the minority in their opposition, they were bound by that agreement and must abide by it."

A new sound swelled from the crowd around Two Crows, throaty knots of disbelief. The grumbling stopped when their speaker took two steps closer to the soldier chief.

"Howard, I understand you to say you have instructions from Washington to move all of us to the reserve. You are always talking about Washington. I would like to know who Washington is. Is he a chief, or a common man, or a house, or a place? Every time you have a council you speak of Washington. Leave Mr. Washington, that is if he is a man, alone. He has no sense. He does not know anything about our country. He was never here."

Howard swept his one arm like a scythe across the crowd gathered before him. "I want all these Indians to go to their reserve at once. If you do not go voluntarily, I will compel you to do so with my soldiers. I have instructions from Washington to move all Indians to their reserves, and according to my instruction I must make you move. If you will not move for my words, you shall go to the reserve by the points of my soldiers' bayonets."

Two Crows' throat tightened before the interpreter finished the general's words. His heart pounded as he tried again to count the soldiers gathered by each door of the barracks and the additional soldiers who had now appeared by the guardhouse. Toolhoolhootzote's voice again focused Two Crow's attention toward the front of the tent.

"The Great Spirit Chief made the world as it is and as he wanted it," Toolhoolhootzote stated in a strong and measured tone, "and he made a part of it for us to live upon. I do not see where you get authority to say that we shall not live where he placed us. What the treaty Indians talk about was born of today. It isn't true law at all. You white people get together and measure the earth and then divide it. What person pretends to divide the land and put me on it?"

For Two Crows, the barracks blurred, the white and black clothing worn by the treaty Nez Perces gathered to the left and right of the council tent blended into a dirty gray, the tent itself became a white cloud against the sky. Two figures filled the scene—one in dark blue cloth with polished brass buttons and gold stars on each shoulder, eyes wide and stormy; the other dressed in brain-tanned buckskin, shoulders draped with strips of beads, eyes the color of deep pools in the shadows of a breaking dawn.

The interpreter cleared his throat, hesitated, recast words into the charged air.

"I am the man," Howard stated in a determined voice. "I stand here for the president, and there is no spirit good or bad that will hinder me. My orders are plain, and they will be executed. I hoped that the Indians had good sense enough to make me their friend and not their enemy."

"Howard, are you trying to scare me?" Toolhoolhootzote's voice was confident and taunting. "Are you going to tell me the day when I will die? I know I must die someday. I have expressed my heart to you. I have nothing to take back. I have spoken for my people."

General Howard's voice was menacing. "Silence! I don't care to hear any more of such talk. The law says you shall go upon the reservation to live, and I want you to do so, but you persist in disobeying the law. If you do not move, I will take the matter into my own hand and make you suffer for your disobedience." The interpreter started to speak, then retreated to an outside corner of the tent and stood nervously near the armed guard stationed there. He directed his voice to the dwindling space separating the general and the chief.

Toolhoolhootzote now pressed his case with defiance. "Who are you, that you ask us to talk and then tell me I am not to talk? Are you the Great Spirit? Did you make the world? Did you make the sun? Did you make the rivers to run for us to drink? Did you make the grass to grow? Did you make all these things that you talk to us as though we were boys? You are trifling with the law of the earth. I never gave any Indians authority to give away the land. I am not going on the reservation!"

The general glanced quickly at the treaty Indians to his left and right, then the non-treaties stiffening before him. The interpreter shared a single sentence with

General Howard. The general's cheeks and forehead flushed, his one arm shook. A single, demanding sound shot from his lips. "Perry!"

An officer moved quickly forward from the rear of the tent. Two Crows parted the side fold in his blanket. His right hand gripped the head of the pipe tomahawk at his belt.

More soldiers appeared at the barracks doors, rifles now in hand. The guards at the front corners of the council tent stretched to their full height as Captain Perry and a second soldier escorted Toolhoolhootzote away.

Chief Thunder-Rolling-Over-The-Mountains stood and turned toward the wave of warriors rising angrily before him. "I am going to talk now," he said in a strong voice. "I don't care whether I am arrested or not. The arrest of Toolhoolhootzote was wrong, but we will not resent the insult. We were invited to this council to express our hearts, and we have done so."

Disbelief at what had happened surged, crested, then broke upon the ground slipping away beneath Two Crows. The one-armed general returned to the front of the council tent. His mouth moved, but Two Crows heard nothing. The general had shown them the rifle. For Two Crows, the council that was not a council was over.

Band by band the non-treaty Nez Perces walked slowly past the guns and the garrison supposedly here for their protection. A wailing song broke the silence as they mounted their horses and rode single file up the valley.

Two Crows joined the rear guard when the non-treaty Nez Perces left the Lapwai, their enemy now behind them, uncertainty ahead. Elders rode grim-faced. Young mothers kept their children within easy reach. For their second sleep, the bands camped by the lake where the giant bones of ancient animals jutted from the mud banks. A rider arrived that evening with the news that on the same day the people had been in council, soldiers had occupied the Wallowa Valley, home of Thunder-Rolling-Over-The-Mountains' band. Anger spread from lodge to lodge, scorching the air like dry grass lightning.

The young men wanted war, ready revenge for the earlier unanswered killing by white men of Willatiah, Tip-piala-natzit-kan, Ta-wai-a-wai-we and Ta-akill-see-waits. Such revenge was the Nez Perce way, their due, their destiny, the young men argued. The old men smoked and talked. They recalled the stories of the first white men who had come to their land many years before. They spoke of how the people had fed these strangers and cared for their horses and agreed to be their friends forever. They talked as well of those who came later—the traders and trappers, the black robes and spirit talkers, the miners, soldiers and settlers—and they tried to understand.

Two Crows felt neither rage nor calm. He had seen fresh blood on a war horse's back, the loose flopping of a dangling arm, brain oozing from a stone-split skull. He had neither the freedom of youth nor the wisdom of age. He was a husband, a father, a warrior. He would know what to do when the time came for the doing.

The next morning he took the back trail, his usual self-assignment of searching for any enemy that might be following. His horse maintained a steady gait as he skirted the white settlement of Cottonwood House, then climbed the rolling benches that defined the base of a mountain that rose into a heavy cloud. Here was one of the mountains to which It'se-ye-ye had tied a rope when he tricked the monster in the Kamiah Valley and created the first two-leggeds for this land, a mountain on which Nez Perce youth for thousands of years had found the guardian spirits of their lives. Two Crows looked for a break in the clouds, hoped for a swath of sunlight burnishing the gold of an eagle's wing or painting a raven purple, but the clouds grew thicker.

He kneed his horse, picking his way amongst the boulders of basalt strewn across diminishing patches of open ground. With the growing odor of horse sweat, he slowed and watched intently for the sign he hoped the mountain would give him. Then the air chilled, and to the southwest the sky turned black with the last throes of an angry spring sweeping out of the Wallowas. Two Crows turned his horse and started his descent.

By the time he reached the front of the whipsawed shack that served as stage station and general store in the six-building settlement of Cottonwood, heavy rain formed puddles in the muddy road. He dismounted and tied his horse to a lodgepole rail. His fingers rubbed the deerskin pouch that hung over the center of his chest as he estimated the amount of fine gold he had received for three horses he had sold to miners the previous fall. White storekeepers, he had learned, were eager to trade anything for the magic dust, and he was in a trading mood.

An hour later and a half-mile from the circles of lodges visible beyond the edge of the advancing storm front, the message from the mountain was confirmed. Two Crows saw men gathering the horse herd, women dismantling lodges, the entire encampment in rapid motion. A rider approached his position, horse's sides heaving. Two young men from White Bird's band had avenged a father's death, the warrior informed him. Joined by a cousin, they had killed four settlers on the Salmon. The time for talk was over, the rider continued. The soldiers would come. The people were moving to a defensive position in White Bird Canyon.

Two Crows kneed his horse to a steady lope, new canvas bag of ammunition bouncing against his thigh.

CHAPTER FOURTEEN

1953

The postcard came when buttercups poked through morning frost on sheltered patches of south-facing earth. The flat-chested grocery clerk whose twin sister worked at the post office told Isaac on a Friday afternoon, said the card had been there for at least a week. Mail of any sort was a rarity in Isaac's life, and General Delivery better than paying for a key and a box of disappointment. It was a plain beige card with a 5-cent stamp printed in one corner and *Isaac Moses* written below in a familiar hand. The message on the back was brief. "Come see me in Pendleton. I want to show you something. Mom" Directions in the lower left corner read "Tutuilla Church Road. Watch for the steeple. Fresh foal in the pasture."

The timing was perfect. Steelhead were holed up and hard to catch. Game was poor, and the roots had not begun to stir in the cold ground. The temporary closure at the mill hung on like winter fog, and spring breakup at higher elevations would soon bring further delays to log trucks rolling into the valley. Cash registers were quiet and chainsaws sat on back porches in shallow pools of oil. Everyone waited for sun, for a break in the gray monotony of a logging town down in winter.

Isaac's knee had continued to mend, stretched by walking the river trail to the railroad bridge and back, packing rounds of red fir to his pickup, sledding elk meat down the slopes of Fish Creek. Twice he'd followed Raven Eye's advice and the snow-packed path to the bank of the Southfork, where steam melted aches and anger alike.

He was eager to see his mother, to show her the tuned-up Ford and the healthy leanness of his face, but the Ford's gas tank was less than half full and he was broke. Many nights he had thought about his hundred dollars scattered on the pawnshop floor, Sheffield wanting him to crawl on his bandaged hand and busted knee to pick it up like a desperate drunk. He had paid his debt, he had decided, and Sheffield would pay his too. Isaac's other money remained hidden in a brick wall behind a yellowed urinal in the Boots & Saddles Bar, a test of his sobriety he had thus far elected to avoid.

His pickup started easily the next morning, a quarter cord of fir in its bed a fair price to pay for a visit with Old Man. When Isaac stepped through the door of Raven Eye's shack with an armload of wood, he was greeted with a song as the tewat rocked rhythmically back and forth on his blanket. "I am thinking of salmon today" Raven Eye said in a singsong style, "They are entering the river. They will follow you home."

Isaac set the wood near the stove and crossed the room to the rocker. He felt comfortable now in its easy swing, its creak on the floor a calming sound that blended with the smell of the wood smoke and the old man and the herbs and furs that hung from nails and pegs in the walls.

"I brought you more elk meat," Isaac announced. "It's in a cooler in my rig. A friend of mine got married and his wife has a freezer. A good thing this time of year."

"You came to see Old Man." Raven Eye smiled with this observation, and Isaac grinned when he replied, "I came to see both old men. Will you join me today?"

"We are all old men in time," said Raven Eye, and he returned to his chant while Isaac rocked and closed his eyes to seal this scene into memory.

They both welcomed their communal visits with Old Man, water hissing into steam, brief streaks of light slicing the mist when Isaac opened the door flap for a breath of cold air, the chill of the river lost once more in the dark heat of the half-dome of their intertwining lives.

Halfway back to Kamiah, Isaac formed his plan. He would go to the bar at 4:30, a Saturday lull between afternoon sops and evening revelers. From the side entrance, he'd take seven steps to the restroom door, flashlight and needle-nosed pliers in his pocket. He'd walk in, walk out, and be gone.

The smoke struck him first, a thick haze that filled the darkest corner of the bar, faces sallow in the barroom light. He strode past unnoticed, reached for the restroom door, gave it a tug, heard the hook catch in the eye. He rattled the door twice to be sure it was locked. He had turned to begin a retreat when Cindy appeared, a well-balanced tray of empties in her hand.

"Isaac, where ya been?" Her raspy voice was earnest. She set her tray on an empty table and slid toward him like a dance partner. "I heard about it," she continued softly, "and then we didn't see you. Thought you was maybe really hurt. He left, ya know, that mean son-of-a-bitch. Down to Nevada I heard. I like your hair long. How about a beer?"

Isaac felt like a rabbit in the gaze of a lynx, at that moment when two paths cross and lives can change in an instant. He heard the click of a latch, and the bathroom light burnished Cindy's teeth, then disappeared with a slap as the restroom door swung shut.

"I gotta hit the john, Cindy," Isaac said with a backward nod of his head. "Save the beer till later." He recalled the night they had spent together years before, her eager warmth, his drunken sleep. He turned, took two quick steps and opened the restroom door.

A run of fresh tobacco juice dribbled down the wall behind the urinal. The hole in the sheetrock was still unpatched. Everything else seemed in its place, wrapped in a well-remembered stench. Isaac latched the door, shined his flashlight into the fist-sized hole and into the crevices of the brick beyond. The barely visible end of a pencil-sized paper roll sprinkled with mortar dust appeared. The needle-nosed pliers worked as planned, and Isaac shoved the bills, flashlight and pliers into his pockets. He fought the sudden urge to pee, unhooked the door, moved quickly across the barroom floor and burst into the day's last sunshine slanting up the south side of Fourth.

Church bells announced an early Mass as Isaac drove across the bridge toward town. His sleeping bag, tightly rolled, lay on the pickup floor. Elk jerky and an assortment of clothing filled a canvas knapsack beside him, USFS stenciled across its flap. West of Kamiah, the winding highway matched the river's curves and bends as it smoothed out the pools and rapids and riffles.

He passed the mouth of Lolo Creek, then the twenty houses with a single bar that clung to the sidehill at the bottom of the Greer Grade. At the south end of the steel-arched bridge that crossed the river to Orofino, he remembered the sports page headlines that still defined his relationship to this town's collection of loggers and lumbermen who rarely missed a hometown game. "Kubs Maul Maniacs" one headline had read, citing Kamiah's team effort built around 28 points and 9 assists for Isaac Moses. A scout from the local university had called the next day wanting to visit with him about Idaho's basketball program, "close to home and good to Indians."

By the time he had passed through Riverside, the growing stiffness in his right knee demanded attention. The mouth of the North Fork across the main stem of the Clearwater drew him shoreward to the meeting place of rivers that had once hosted thousands of people and millions of salmon, "almost as big as Celilo," Raven Eye had told him. A grassy patch among the pines made a convenient turnout. A roadside sign declared this the place where Meriwether Lewis and William Clark and their Corps of Discovery had made dugout canoes to travel to the sea, thousands of years of Nez Perce history ignored in the sign's carefully crafted story.

At Big Eddy, the river circled and churned, and the hills were bare of trees by the time he made the bend at Myrtle. By now his leg ached, and Spalding Park invited another stretch, the well-trimmed grounds clear testimony to the park's official status. On the far side of the park, a board and batten cabin leaned slightly toward the river. A dugout canoe stretched across much of the cabin's weathered facade. Isaac pulled into the parking lot, slipped the gearshift into neutral and braked the Ford with his left foot. As the pickup slid in the gravel and jerked to a stop, a man emerged from the cabin door, watched Isaac step gingerly from the pickup cab and smiled a greeting. "She came from Kamiah," he said as Isaac walked to the dugout, straightening his right leg with every other step. "Ya know, Lewis & Clark made a dugout in Kamiah, did it in the spring on their return trip. Lost it there in the current. Maybe this is the one. She's old. Worth a lot."

Isaac paced off the dugout as he walked its length, 38 feet of cedar shovel-nosed at the ends, a narrow split on one side.

"I'm not usually open this time of year, just today for the Boy Scouts at their camporee over there." The man gestured toward a flat between the road and a hillside to the south. "Rained hard last night, scooted them under that bridge in a hurry. Come on inside. I'll show you some real stuff." He studied Isaac's face, then added matter-of-factly, "Everybody likes Indian stuff, they just don't all like Indians."

Isaac ducked through the narrow door and was immediately surrounded by the largest collection of beads and buckskin, fans and baskets, stone tools, quivers and drums he had ever imagined. A pawnbroker's dream, he thought to himself, in oak and glass cases, on top of cases, in boxes stacked in the corners, and hanging from nails pounded into the rough-sawn studs and joists.

"Each piece could tell a story," the man continued as Isaac's heart began to drum in his chest. "The good stuff is disappearing, and the stories will follow."

Isaac couldn't speak. He turned to his right and his eyes began deliberately sweeping the scene in a counterclockwise direction. Here were his people, boxed and shelved and hung, all in this small back eddy building at the edge of a monument to missionaries who had rent the fabric of Nez Perce culture. He stood suspended in the middle of a message he didn't understand. Yet its power gripped him, held him, only gradually allowed him to breath again as he completed the visual circle and stepped toward the door.

"You feeling okay?" the man asked as Isaac passed through the door. Isaac made no reply. He paused at his pickup, started to get in, decided instead to circle the park, to walk off the tightness that had spread upwards from his knee like wildfire, his lungs demanding the dampness of soft rain and spring air.

Across the road the smoky fires of the uniformed campers clouded the space beneath a concrete bridge over railroad tracks. Beyond the smoke, rows of headstones filled an opening amongst the maples, stone testimony to the faithful work of Henry and Eliza Spalding. Isaac walked, then stopped beside the missionaries' own memorial, its six-foot grandeur perhaps requiring the hand of God himself in its placement. Lichens licked at the edges of the letters chiseled there, but the message remained. *Coming as the morning sun over the mountains in response to the historic search of the Nez Perces for the White man's book of heaven, they dispelled the darkness of this once benighted race and gave to them the light of life.* Isaac mouthed those words again and again, each time sliding deeper into his own form of darkness. He took large breaths as he halted under a bare-limbed locust that afforded no protection from a passing shower, then fled with a ragged running motion, right leg barely able to follow his left leg's pace. Parallel to his awkward jog laid the railroad track and soon the sign that proclaimed another dot on the trail on which he traveled. "Spalding" was painted in bold letters on the signpost beside the wooden shelter that served as a depot, with three steps leading to the platform. A bench filled the length of the station, and Isaac sat while rain dripped off the roofline and shined the tracks before him. He closed his eyes, his breathing slowed, his sense of panic subsided. He knew that this place, too, was a part of the stitching together of the visions and voices of his life.

Here his mother had met his father when they were traveling their own paths home. He sat until the shower quit, then followed the tracks and slippery ties past the Boy Scouts huddled in their wet-wood smoke.

A dozen miles west, Highway 12 joined 95 at the bottom of Lewiston's Spiral Hill. The Colonial Motel sat in the forks, white with blue trim above a freshly mowed lawn. Isaac turned left, passed a row of bars abandoned on a Sunday morning, crossed the river to the center of town. D Street led him past the Lewis & Clark Hotel. A second bridge carried him over the Snake River into Washington. With scattered businesses along Clarkston's Bridge Street soon in his rearview mirror, he was once again rushing west with the spring melt, the river wild and strong beside him.

He stopped to stretch at Alpowa Summit, where green sprouts of winter wheat carpeted the hillsides. Pomeroy was next, which passed like a glance, and with mouth dry from sucking jerky, he stopped in Dayton for gas and a Pepsi, with change enough for a bag of peanuts and a double wrap of Twinkies.

He missed the turn to Pendleton just west of Walla Walla while watching a redtail swooping over stubble. The first opportunity to turn around came at a side road to Wailatpu, once home to missionaries Dr. Marcus and Narcissa Whitman. Here in freshly painted letters were finally Indians in the drama of the white man's west, Cayuse killers of the missionaries who had come to save the Indians' benighted souls.

His mood was flat as he descended into the shallow valley of the Umatilla where Pendleton's commerce clustered at the bottom of the draw and houses climbed the hills on either side. The sign that pointed to the main road south identified the route as the Oregon Trail. Once again a stranger, he pulled his mother's folded postcard from his shirt pocket and reminded himself of the route to the rez. "Tutuilla Church Road. Watch for the steeple. Fresh foal in the pasture." He left the highway before Emigrant Hill, drove slowly by the houses and horses and occasional pile of stacked tipi poles reaching skyward, to Tutuilla Road, where a steeple drew him north. The church was Presbyterian, a blocky bell tower on the side as if an afterthought. Curves of glass arched over the double entry doors tried unsuccessfully to soften the building's angular lines. A cemetery lay on a nearby rise. A short way west three cottonwoods shaded a plain plank house beside a fenced pasture with two mares and an appaloosa filly. The Chevy pickup parked in the front yard was dead, its engine hanging from a tripod of poles, its hood leaning against a weathered corral. Isaac switched off the Ford's engine and visually searched for signs of his mother among a medley of wooden boxes in the dusty yard. The house door opened and a young woman stepped onto a makeshift porch.

"You must be Isaac," she said. "Your mom told me you'd come in an old green Ford."

Isaac glanced at her long black hair, the curves of her checkered blouse, the smile that slowly spread across her angled face. He smiled in return.

"She's gone to the falls," the woman continued. "She wants you to meet her there. They're killing the river, you know. It's the buffalo all over again." She paused for a moment, glanced briefly into Isaac's eyes, started a slow turn towards the open door. "Get your gear and come on in," she added as she nodded toward his pickup. "I've got some venison stew on the stove."

CHAPTER FIFTEEN

1836

The dream's appearance was unpredictable, creeping into Runs-Like-A-Deer's sleep on thickly padded paws. The smell of moist breath was always followed by a glimpse of teeth and yellow eyes with a slice of moon on the pupils' upper edges. Runs-Like-A-Deer shook awake, then dressed in the faint light of the longhouse as a woman stirred near a smoldering fire two families away. The rawhide flap of the nearest exit brushed his shoulder as he stepped into a summer dawn.

His brief walk up a timbered ridge ended on a grassy hillside wet with dew. A goshawk swooped a warning. A band of horses appeared from a thin mist, passed out of view as they dipped into a creek bottom, then halted on a bunchgrass slope. Seven horses would be enough for the journey, he decided, eyeing the grazing stock—three to ride, three to pack and a spare in case of a lame leg or bruised frog. A two-year-old colt sprinted past, a rusty roan with white leggings and black-spotted withers. Eight horses, he decided, this one a gift for his boyhood friend, Daytime Smoker, who lived with the Salish on the eastern side of the mountains.

Runs-Like-A-Deer had been a child of the village, his mother a medicine woman, his father a mystery. His grandparents died of the stinking disease many years before he was born, his mother, Two Stars, had told him, in that terrible time when whole villages vanished. His father had come from the east with strangers, stayed one moon and never returned. He was a swift runner and had a good heart, she frequently added.

He caught a friendly mare, rode slowly across the grassy flat beside the bend of the river where an ancient lodge ring pocked the earth amongst thinly scattered pines. Swollen with mountain snowmelt, the river swirled at the base of cottonwoods lining its edge. Shoots of willow and dogbane bent west with the current. The ground on which he rode had been hallowed by the bones of hundreds of generations of his people folded into the earth. The grass was itself ancestral.

Midsummer would not be the first fur rendezvous for Runs-Like-a-Deer, or the second, or the third. He had traveled several years to distant forks and holes and valleys where traders and trappers gathered, had reveled in the horse racing, the gambling, the dancing, the constant bartering and bantering that briefly glued the tribes and trappers together. His mother would be there as well and would walk once more among the white men's lodges, search their faces, show the trappers her pipe tomahawk with five blue beads embedded in its handle and ask again about the man who had briefly, unforgettably, slipped into and out of her life.

This year's rendezvous would be her last, she had told her son. The spirit talkers were her interest now. Word had been relayed from band to band across the buffalo plains that white man spirit talkers were coming to Nez Perce country, teachers who could capture talk on thin skin with a stick and share the white man's *wyakin*, the source of all his power.

At the end of the moon of cous bread, Runs-Like-A-Deer, his wife Wren Song, Two Stars and others from their village crossed the mountains on crusted snow, their horses' hooves sinking fetlock deep by late afternoon. Forty-five strong, for three days they stopped only to eat, sleep and graze their 120 head of bays, paints and buckskins on south-facing slopes where beargrass blossoms waved their musky scent into the open weave of mountain air. The fourth day the men smoked the pipe on a ridge-top knoll near a cairn of stones from which a pine pole pointed to the sky. That evening a wolf howled from the mountain top above their camp, solitary and searching.

On the sixth day, the party camped where chokecherries lined the banks of the creek they had followed east to the Bitterroot River. Here Daytime Smoker found them. Late day sun highlighted the red tint of his yellow braids as he rode into the Nez Perce camp leading a handsome paint. He and Runs-Like-A-Deer visited into the night while their gifts to each other grazed on a grassy bench nearby.

Their numbers grew as the travelers rode up the valley, a family here, a small group there, tributaries feeding a swelling stream. A band of Salish joined them where It'se-ye-ye once tricked an angry ram into embedding its horns in a pine tree trunk. Strips of cloth decorated shoots of ninebark near the base of the giant pine. The scent of tobacco hovered above the ram's horn protruding from the ponderosa's deeply creviced bark. Two days later they crossed the divide, and by late afternoon their trailing horse herd fanned out on a grassy bottom soon dotted with buffalo skin lodges, columns of smoke blending with a graying sky. Here was the Big Hole, resting stop of generations. Wrapped in easy familiarity, the people ate, visited and danced.

Four days later they pitched their camp beside Horse Creek two miles above its entrance to the Green River. From a band of Bannocks camped nearby, Runs-Like-A-Deer learned that the traders' caravan was one day out.

A line of moving dots appeared the next afternoon through the resin-soaked air that hovered over summer hot sage, and Runs-Like-A-Deer joined the welcoming party—part trapper, part Indian, and all curiosity. The greeters fired their rifles into the air as they galloped down both sides of a single line of mounted traders, 400 mules and packhorses strung out like a giant snake slithering over the sandy soil. At the rear of the train the boisterous greeters discovered six mules pulling a wagon, its steel-rimmed wheels turning a narrow track. Beside the wagon, two women rode sidesaddle, their dusty white faces bobbing with each step of their mounts.

Yards of fabric flared from their waists. The first looked gaunt, skin stretched taut by months and miles. The second appeared round and robust. Runs-Like-A-Deer slowed his horse to a walk. His eyes followed the turn of the wheels and the movements of the women beside them.

A mile further, the caravan halted. As soon as the white women's boots found ground, Nez Perce women surrounded the pair. Brown fingers brushed the fabric of the women's dresses, the stitching of a hem, the polished curve of a hairpiece. The Nez Perces greeted, inspected, chattered and moved on. They were followed by a flock of Salish women, then several Snakes. Two Stars arrived with the next wave. She studied the white women's faces, their clothing, their hands. She touched a scarf around Eliza Spalding's neck, shell buttons on Narcissa Whitman's dress. She lingered, drawn to the tint of red in the blond curls above the latter's trail-stained collar, hair the color of a late day sun sprinkled with morning coals.

Trappers came next, long away from Kentucky mothers or St. Louis sisters or hometown lovers. They stared and smiled. Some tipped their hats. Most added a glance at the two husbands of the main attraction, gave more time to the fifteen head of beef and milk cows accompanying the missionary party before departing for the predicted center of the American Fur Company camp. Traps and trade goods were their principal interest—tobacco and tea, sugar and salt, calico and whiskey. They knew the jamboree would soon begin.

Later that day in an elk skin lodge at the western edge of the Nez Perce camp, Two Stars spoke to her son. She was through inquiring about his father, she explained, now just a pleasant memory. But here was opportunity, she stated calmly, referring to the woman with hair the same color as the braids that framed the face of Daytime Smoker, her son's childhood friend. Two Stars handed her son a buckskin bag, the band of quillwork near its top frayed and faded. Runs-Like-A-Deer understood and nodded his agreement.

Five men sat in a circle beside the four-wheeled wagon when Runs-Like-A-Deer approached. The caravan chief, Broken Hand, was talking quietly to a hawk-beaked man with a black silk scarf around his neck and a black mustache above his freshly shaven chin. The man called Gabe sat between Broken Hand and a trapper, Doc, who was married to a Nez Perce woman. A fifth man sitting opposite Gabe was unknown to Runs-Like-A-Deer. Passing gracefully among them capturing their attention, Narcissa Whitman dispensed hot tea and smiles. Doc stirred at Runs-Like-A-Deer's approach, spoke softly to the hostess, who then signaled for Runs-Like-A-Deer to join them.

"Yes, the spirit talkers are coming to Nez Perce country," the woman stated with a quiet determination likely lost in the translation provided by Doc Newell in response to Runs-Like-A-Deer's question. "Yes, their wives will come with them," she added. "They are bringing the book as promised," Doc continued, his ease with the Nez Perce language apparent, "and she says they will stay a long time."

Runs-Like-A-Deer looked directly at Doc Newell. "Does this white woman know the red-headed chief who lives by the big river?" he asked in his native tongue. Doc Newell replied "She does not," and the group's conversation would have moved on but for the woman's inquiry as to the nature of Runs-Like-A-Deer's question. Newell responded to her, and the matter appeared settled when Gabe motioned to the man sitting across from him and said in Salish, "This man knows the red-headed chief." The man Gabe had referred to straightened his wiry form from its forward lean and brushed away the straight black hair that hung down the sides of his face.

Runs-Like-A-Deer removed a pipe-tomahawk from the buckskin bag his mother had given him earlier in the day. He held the pipe in front of his chest and faced the man now watching him intently. "Do you know the man who carried this pipe when he traveled with the red-headed chief to the sea?"

Doc Newell translated to the man, who responded to Runs-Like-A-Deer with the sign for "no."

Runs-Like-A-Deer glanced at Newell. "The man I ask about helped our people understand the white men's talk." Another exchange occurred between Newell and the stranger, and the others in the circle turned their heads toward each speaker in turn.

"Two interpreters were on that journey," Doc Newell advised Runs-Like-A-Deer. "One was this man's father," he added.

Runs-Like-A-Deer measured the stranger carefully—his hands, his face, the spread of his shoulders, the cant of his legs. "The man I ask about was a swift runner," Runs-Like-A-Deer explained to Newell, "the fastest man in the party."

Again the trappers, traders and woman turned their heads toward the man who had become the center of inquiry. "Drouillard," came his reply to Doc Newell. "He was killed by Blackfoot near the Three Forks many years ago."

The American Fur Company cracked the first keg of whiskey in the center of their camp shortly after the evening meal. The company's only teetotaler was put in charge of sales, and the grizzled trappers began to shed their annual catch and any inhibitions that might have strayed with them out of the mountains. Campfires flared nearby, and soon the waves of greasy buckskin flowing across the prairie were joined by new attire covered with quills, beads and baubles. Drumbeats rippled across the night, and the revelers absorbed the rawhide's rhythm.

Runs-Like-A-Deer joined the carnival scene. He drummed the top of a hollow log and chanted as a tattooed bone passed from hand to hand. He cheered the betting, won a quiver, traded for a knife, and gambled away a bow. He shared in the frequent rounds of a salt-clay jug and the annual gaiety of mountain men. Finally his legs grew weak, the faces around him blurred. He stumbled to a trickle of a creek that bordered a willow patch beyond the campfire light. He knelt to drink.

Just before his lips touched water, he smelled an animal's moist breath, turned his head and glimpsed white teeth and yellow eyes, felt fur brush his cheek and neck. Sharp pain ripped through his shoulder and spread like a flame across his back as a crescent moon cleared a single cloud scudding across the sky.

CHAPTER SIXTEEN

1953

Tumbleweeds scurried across the dry plateau west of Pendleton, then piled up in obedient rows against the barbed wire fence that paralleled the highway. Isaac had lingered on Tutuilla Road, had sipped a second cup of boiled coffee after breakfast. Bernice's evening smile went missing somewhere between white bread and bacon, her voice stretched tightly over the framework of her argument—the dams and the salmon, the buffalo and the Indian, the white man's constant need to destroy the land. Isaac watched her bite her lower lip between bundles of sentences tied neatly together, well edited and rehearsed. She was a dreamer and believer, he had decided, not of the old ways but of the future, a woman bending anger into action, her voice transformed in the process.

He twisted the steering wheel into gusts hitting the side of the pickup as roadside teasel bent sharply north.

His people had come here for centuries, Bernice had reminded him. They had crossed this sagebrush seabed on trails wider than this highway, to Celilo Falls, where millions of salmon stitched the earth together threading their way upstream.

By mid-morning the broad Columbia came into view. The river looked calm in the distance, then restless as Isaac drew nearer. He stopped at the first highway turnout to stretch his leg and greet the river. Here the water from thousands of springs, creeks and rivers mingled—from the Lochsa and Selway, the Coeur d'Alene and Spokane, from British Columbia to Jackson's Hole—all trickling, running and rushing toward Celilo, long-time gathering place of the people and the salmon. "Wyam," Bernice had said, "first village below Deschutes, on the Oregon side," explaining where Isaac's mother would likely be. "She'll be helping Peter Jack, getting the platforms ready and stuff. Four more weeks and they'll be here."

Isaac wasn't sure what Bernice meant by "stuff," but he knew it was the salmon whose arrival was so eagerly anticipated. The fish meant fresh food and cash after a long winter and offered reassurance that the rhythm of the land was still in place, the spirits pleased, earth's promise fulfilled.

From beneath the blue bandanna atop his mother's weathered face, a smile welcomed Isaac. His hug was comfort, hers was joy. In one embrace they dispelled the past two years of absence. Peter Jack had gone to the coast for two weeks' work, Isaac's mother explained, but she had waited at Celilo confident that Isaac would come. She was glad he had met Bernice, “a good woman, but she sometimes gets a fish bone caught in her throat,” she told him. She thought the Ford looked good. She glanced at the ragged scar on Isaac’s cheek but didn’t ask. “The river,” she finally said, “I wanted you to see the river.”

The village was a jumble of houses and fish racks, gear shacks tucked here and there, cars and pickups, weeds and random dogs. Dipnets, ropes and fish boxes lined weathered porches, and people nodded and smiled as mother and son passed by.

Mary gathered lunch from inside her camper trailer parked at the edge of the village while Isaac retrieved his clothes and bedroll from the Ford. They visited on the walk to the river—Kamiah and the spotted filly, snow pack and mourning doves, Mary’s part-time job in Pendleton. The level ground on which they walked ended abruptly at the edge of steep bluffs that dropped two hundred feet to the water. A short way upstream the run-off from a hundred thousand square miles of mountains and meadows, wind-scoured scablands, canyons, prairies and plateaus all squeezed itself into half the river’s usual width above a crescent-shaped ledge and plunged. White foam frothed and boiled. Sunlight scattered images of stained glass across thick patches of mist rising toward a pale blue sky.

Mary motioned toward a cleft in the rock a few yards below, and they descended carefully and sat. With the noise of the river, speech was impractical, impossible, unwanted. Platforms and scaffolding clung to the cliffs—planks, posts and beams nailed, bolted, fitted and cabled to the basalt, suspended over rushing water rising now each day. Chief Island, Tumwater, The Roping Place and Hobo Rock—all were here on the river in this gathering place of the people celebrating life with the salmon's rich flesh and one another. Isaac and his mother huddled against the rock, Mary gesturing toward the white walls of water, the black basalt, the blue-green curves and twists upstream where the river readied itself for the falls.

She cupped her left hand between her mouth and the river and shouted to him, "This is what I wanted you to see, before it's all gone."

Spotting a niche lower on the bluff, Isaac started down the rough basalt, toes reaching, hands clinging. He thought he heard his mother's voice call "tie-off rope," the river drowning out all other sound. He was soon hugging the rocks like a fishing platform, arms and legs jammed into cracks, butt anchored on a tiny shelf. He sat mesmerized by the water, by this place, and then the roar disappeared and the play began, just as Raven Eye had described it. Men appeared on anchored platforms, upstream, downstream, sweeping the water with long handled dipnets in a synchronous dance. The dancers sang—to the water, to the earth, to the silvery shapes that surged upstream. The men's voices joined the river's song, and Isaac's mind captured mid-air a thousand leaping salmon in a colored tintype still life.

He suddenly felt an urge to join the river, a giving in more than a giving up, allowing gravity its due. He recalled that fishermen fell sometimes from their platforms or were pulled into the river by giant fish in the current, or lured to the depths by the liquid arms of maidens. He could just let go, he thought, could join the shimmering silvery horde, could cast himself like molten metal into every hollow of this exquisite scene.

A rope interrupted the singing, the dream—brown hemp, store bought, touching his left shoulder, then slithering down his left arm and coiling on the crevice where he'd wedged the heel of his left foot. A patch of moss beneath his right heel sloughed downhill, and Isaac dug the fingers of his right hand harder into a narrow crack in the basalt. He knew he had to act, to thread that line around his waist and tie a lasting knot with a single hand. He tried a bowline, settled on a timber hitch, felt his right leg sliding as the knot tightened just below his ribs. The rope became taut and began lifting him from his perch. He grabbed the rope with both hands, turned uphill and pushed against the rocks with sliding feet. He could see two men above him, backs bent, legs set, faces stretched. His mother peered over the edge, frown deep and smile wide, and soon he was on his knees on flat ground, and they all laughed and caught their breaths and laughed again.

Mother and son walked the beach upstream from the village and sat on a driftwood log to eat their lunch and talk.

"The white men thought they were listening, but they just couldn't hear us," declared Mary after telling her son how the elders had tried to explain to the Army Corps of Engineers the meaning of Celilo. "They've started the digging, giant Cats busting up ancient village sites, dynamite throwing huge rocks into the air.

I wanted you to see it, not that, but this, the chutes, the falls, fishermen roped to the rocks, the dipnets and the drying fish. They're still trying to kill us, Isaac. It's just like Carlisle. Now they're going to drown us with our own river."

Isaac winced at the mention of Carlisle, slid off the log and straightened his right leg. He faced his mother, hoping this break would punctuate her sentence and shift their conversation in a new direction.

"I heard about the beating," she continued. "Lucy Bowen came through last month. She didn't know the details, said you were holed up as usual, probably all right. Do you still have the Carlisle ledger book, Isaac? Bernice says that's an important record. It needs to be kept safe."

Isaac brushed his beating aside, said as calmly as he could, "It's in a safe place, Mom."

"Are you sweating that leg of yours?" she asked. "Your grandmother would use nettles. Draws the blood to the damage."

"I've been going up to Stites, to an old man there. It's good."

Mary studied her son's lean face, his uncut hair touching the top of his shirt pocket, his eyes squinting in the sun. "You're visiting the tewat?" she asked, her tone flat.

"Yes. Raven Eye. He's teaching me the old ways."

Mary looked upstream, started to speak, stumbled on the first word and stopped.

"My grandmother," Isaac began after a long silence. "Did she come to Celilo?"

"I don't think so." Mary answered. "She liked a lot of solitude."

"I went by my father's grave last week." Isaac looked at his mother again, a sudden touch of sadness at the corners of her eyes. "And yesterday I tried to see the two of you at Spalding, at the train platform, where you told me you had met—you remember, the letter and all, his army uniform on a summer day. I could see you there with a pretty smile. He was just a shadow."

They sat in silence, sand in the crevices of the driftwood log coarse against the seats of their jeans, the usual afternoon breeze beginning to stir.

"He was a soldier, Isaac, young and strong. Handsome too. He loved horses, raced on the flat by the railroad bridge. The Dreamers buried him before you were born." Mary stood, smiled an end to this visit on a cedar log that could have come from Kamiah or Coeur d'Alene, a gift for the longhouse waiting to be sawed and split, kindling for the smoke, the prayers and the stories. They walked back to the village, the breeze upriver stronger now, a touch of sand in the air.

"They're working near Skein now. Big Cats and big crews ripping the earth apart," Mary told him. "I'll get dinner started."

Isaac drove out of the village at dawn hoping to find the dozers still, morning air pure, the cooing of mourning doves announcing the coming of the salmon. A cloud of dust and diesel smoke told him he was already late, and after another mile he followed a short dirt road to a willow patch beside the river and parked. Upstream the Columbia split among islands, dove through channels, then pooled and sprawled flat, quiet and spent. On the other side of this liquid calm, D-8s bucked and belched, jammed their giant blades into the shoreline ripping up portage trails, dipnet sites and ancient pigment painted on slabs of stone older than the river itself.

He thought of his mother and his people watching the river rise over chutes and islands, falls and fishing platforms, villages and gravesites. Anger rose in his chest, flushed his neck and cheeks, struggled with the depression that clouded his mind, leaving him anchored to the seat of his pickup. A redheaded blackbird scolding from a cattail clump broke his spell. He dropped the Ford's gearshift into reverse and backed to a wide spot in the road, then turned his back on what he had witnessed. *It's the buffalo all over again.* Bernice's words filled his head throughout the drive back to Wyam.

He stopped to tell his mother goodbye over hot coffee and warm oatmeal in a plastic bowl, his legs jammed under the Formica top of the camper table. Her talk was heartfelt, with the usual tinge of loss at the departure of her son. She wished he would stay longer but was glad he had come. Celilo was a special place, Bernice was a good woman, single too, but mostly she had wanted to see him, to know he was safe, was not killing himself slowly in the company of cowards.

He hugged her in the doorway, said he'd try to come again when the platform dancers dipped their nets and the river ran thick with salmon. She stood framed in trailer door trim, sad and smiling and beautiful.

"There's something you should know, Isaac," Mary said, looking at the ground between them as her son backed towards his pickup. She lifted her head, leveled her eyes on his. "Raven Eye is my mother's brother, Isaac. Raven Eye is your uncle."

Three days after settling back into the shadows of his cabin, Isaac drove through Kooskia, crossed the South Fork at Stites and braked in his usual spot in front of Raven Eye's house.

"It's your nephew, back from Celilo," Isaac stated in a steady tone, his voice aiding the old man's squinting eye in the poorly lit room.

Raven Eye studied his visitor's stance, his face, his hands, but he did not speak.

"Shall I sit down?" Isaac inquired.

Raven Eye tilted his head like he might be sniffing the air trying to identify danger. "I need some mules ear roots," he began, "not arrowleaf, but mules ear. Do you know where to find some?" He told Isaac where the warmest hillsides would be this time of year, described the crowding of the long, wide leaves on the stem.

Raven Eye rocked slowly on his blanket. "Come back tomorrow and we'll steam."

"I'll bring the roots in the morning," Isaac responded as he turned toward the door.

On the drive back to Kamiah his mother's inquiry about the Carlisle ledger book weighed on Isaac like a long winter's snow load on a deserted trapper cabin. He started to turn toward his driveway, hooked left instead and crossed the bridge into town. As he drove slowly past the pawnshop, a part of him hoped to see the "Closed" sign in the window, but it was not there. He turned right on Fourth and parked, retraced his route on foot and paused at the bottom of the concrete steps that led to the pawnshop entrance. The door opened as the sound of dance bells nailed to an inside panel announced another trade, a sale, a birth or death, a grocery bill or the bottom of a bottle in a brown paper bag.

"He's bad today." The woman's face was tightly drawn, wrapped in braids that disappeared beneath a black shawl. "Be careful," she advised as she passed Isaac at the bottom of the steps. He watched her turn north, wondered if she needed a ride, climbed the steps, shook the bells hard as he opened the door and let the game begin.

From behind the showcase countertops, Bill Sheffield turned quickly toward this boldness bursting into his shop, narrowed his eyes, raised his hands halfway up his sides amidst the mixed odors of fresh whiskey and stale cigar smoke. Isaac wasn't sure how to read Sheffield's arms, but he'd seen those eyes before, hard and unforgiving.

"Ya got a tough look today, Isaac, and you came to the right place." The pawnbroker's voice was raspy, his words reckless. Like two wolves at a territory's edge, each man stared and studied.

Isaac started to speak, but was cut off by a Sheffield snarl. "The ledger book is gone, so get your ass out of here."

Eyes still locked, Isaac took one step towards the slot of space between the two display cases. The iron grate to the back room vault was open just enough for a man to enter. Sheffield lowered his right arm as he passed his cluttered desk. Turning left to face Isaac square on, he raised a .45 Colt belt high, gun hand close to the oval beaded buckle he always wore.

All motion stopped. All sound ceased. Neither man breathed.

Isaac lowered his gaze to the gaping end of the .45, turned slowly toward the door and smiled.

CHAPTER SEVENTEEN

1836

A pastel dawn traced the welted seams of buffalo hides high above Wren Song's face, an invitation to rise, stir the coals, coax a flame with shredded bark and offer a prayer for the new day. She rolled onto her left side, right shoulder rubbing the soft pile of the Hudson's Bay blanket covering her. As her right hand stretched across the course black hair of bear hide she had restlessly removed during the night, the smell of blood flared her nostrils. She slid her hand down the smooth curve of her right hip, felt the dry length of her inner thighs. She reached across the bear hide robe, was surprised to feel her husband clothed as her hand gently climbed his buckskin-clad back. At the round of his shoulder her movement stopped. His shirt was ripped, a wide tear extending from his neck past the bottom of his shoulder blade. Her fingers became warm and sticky. Wren Song sat up quickly, blanket pooling in her naked lap.

When she touched him again, Runs-Like-A-Deer stirred. With the tips of her fingers she explored the length of his arm, his chest, his neck, his face. He sat up and glanced around the interior of the lodge as if trying to determine where he was.

Wren Song helped him remove his shirt, and in the light that began to seep through the tipi's walls, she cleaned his shoulder and the base of his neck with its two round holes and a strip of muscle split and torn. She packed the wounds with ginger root and covered them with a layer of brain-tanned hide from an unborn fawn. He had had a dream, offered her husband as his only explanation, and he had not been able to run.

She was sewing her husband's shirt on the shaded side of the lodge when the news arrived in their camp and scattered like a covey of startled quail. When last night's liquor had been watered down for the third time and the final stick game had ended, when white trappers, traders and Indians lay in brotherly heaps by dying fires, a visitor had passed among them. Blacker than the night, reported those who had glimpsed the beast, with eyes the color of flames. Silent and fearless, the creature had paused occasionally to sink its frothy teeth into a bare arm or leg extending from a buffalo robe. A friend of Gabe's had been bitten on the neck, and the one-eyed trapper who wintered with the Crow was limping with a torn calf. Nine men in all had been sewn together by the spirit talker medicine man. The village crier declared only men with white blood had been attacked. The age-old agreement between wolf and Indian remained intact.

The destination of the spirit talkers soon returned as the major topic of conversation among the Indians. The entire Nez Perce delegation had concluded that the missionaries were meant to settle amongst them, that these were the people promised when four of their tribe had traveled to Chief Red Head's town on the big river where the sun first rises in the morning. This was the promise, too, of the white medicine man called Whitman at the previous year's rendezvous. Each day the Nez Perces watched the missionaries' camp for signs of packing and readied themselves to lead the spirit talkers across the mountains to the Nez Perce homeland. The Cayuse and Salish made their own appeals, describing the advantages of their respective lands and their eagerness to learn of the white man's god.

Hudson's Bay Company postponed a resolution to the ensuing competition. Hoping to purchase a few stray furs, a band of company men appeared when the American whiskey was gone. The British brigade planned to travel to Fort Hall on the Snake River Plain, they told the missionaries, then on to their outpost on the Walla Walla River. The missionaries decided to join them.

Ten sleeps after the opening night of the rendezvous, Wren Song lashed her last parfleche to a second packhorse and she and the camp began flowing west. In the lead were the King's men with their rifles sheathed, relaxed with the numbers of their expanded party. Next rode the spirit talkers, wearing down with every turn of their wagon's squeaking wheels long out of grease, pushing the wagon across creeks and up sagebrush slopes with the determination of true believers.

Next rode the Nez Perce, the Cayuse and the Salish—helping occasionally with the wagon, sharing dried meat with the spirit talkers and constantly observing these promised ones among them. The string of riders stretched for half a mile, dust rising from the sandy soil of the high plateau that defined much of their route.

Each morning Wren Song watched her husband riding at the caravan's edge, shoulders slumped, gazing at the ground. Each evening when the dogs had settled and the ash of cooking fires had turned clay gray, he would appear through the door of their lodge and slip quietly beneath the sleeping robe Wren Song readied at the end of each day's march. He no longer turned toward her, strong and eager. He seldom spoke. He would leave before dawn, a shadow slipping into and out of her life.

Every day she watched the wagon, it's narrow wheels etching a trail through the desert landscape. Like the rest of her people, she knew that the *chick-chick-shauile-kai-kash* could not go over the mountains to their country, the width of its wheels too great for mountain travel. They waited for the spirit talkers to grow tired of the wagon or for the *chick-chick* to break down and be abandoned.

The party reached Bear River on the fifth day of their travels. Here Black Coat, the spirit talker who frequently frowned, held a council for the entire camp. Holding his sacred book, he spoke through a translator about a white man tewat who had died for two suns and come back to life. The Indians understood this talk, for they also had tewats who had died and come back to life.

And like Nez Perce tewats, the white man's tewat spoke with spirits, healed people and prescribed special ceremonies to ward off evil. Black Coat added that the white man's god spoke through the black book and was the only god worthy of their attention.

The next day, convinced that the spirit talkers were not coming to their land, the Salish struck north toward Three Forks and buffalo country. American trappers joined them with their year's supply of tobacco, tea and trading cloth. The rest of the train pushed steadily west, pausing occasionally when the *chick-chick* became stuck in a creek or upset on the side of a steep slope.

The white woman with mouse brown hair talked with Wren Song before each day's march or after lodges had been set up in late afternoon. The woman would point to a copper kettle, a beargrass basket, a lodge, a fire. Wren Song would say a single word each time the woman pointed. The woman sucked each word like a ripe chokecherry and repeated each as if trying to spit out a pit. She was wearing thin, growing tired and sick. Wren Song gave her camas bread and hawthorn tea, and one day a hug. Mouse-hair smiled and hugged her back.

The Nez Perces debated their position as the party approached a major fork in the trail where the fur men had built a lodge of hewn logs and sun-baked mud. The white medicine man would not give up the *chick-chick*, which he had modified to a two-wheeled cart when the front axle had splintered on sharp basalt protruding from the desert floor. Black Coat was angry much of the time. The woman with hair the color of warm coals was sick every morning. The mouse-haired one was sick all day. The spirit talkers' cattle were sore-footed, and a cow with a wound on its left hind leg had begun to bawl incessantly.

The afternoon of the following day the cow with the worsening limp refused to ford a creek. Herd boys chased it back to the crossing and lashed its rump with their horsehair quirts. The worn-out Guernsey stood her ground, dusty legs anchored in the sand. Her lower jaw hung slack. Flecks of foam spewed from nostrils flared with heavy breathing. She bellowed into the hot desert air.

The *chick-chick* stopped, and the spirit talker medicine man stepped off the wagon seat. He walked between the parallel tracks that marked the cart's grinding progress and waded the creek. He approached the bawling animal with a cautious curiosity, then quickly returned to his cart. A trapper appeared from the fur brigade, paused to speak to the white medicine man, spurred his mount to the creek and crossed. With casual ease he lifted a long-barreled pistol from his waistband and extended his right arm. Acrid smoke and thunder froze all nearby movement except for the splaying of the Guernsey's buckling legs.

That night Wren Song dreamed a familiar hand touched her breasts, slid down the curve of her waist, crossed the growing roundness of her belly. At first light she remembered the dream when her arm touched the cold steel of her husband's rifle, its octagon barrel nestled into bear hide. Beside it laid his powder horn, brass base dull with oxidation, and his steel dagger with three metal rivets through the polished antler handle. A row of five blue beads lent the only color to this collection, imbedded in the curly-maple handle of a pipe tomahawk touching the dagger's tip.

Wren Song knew she would never see Runs-Like-A-Deer again.

CHAPTER EIGHTEEN

1953

A veil of smoke shrouded the cottonwoods near Raven Eye's sweat lodge when Isaac pulled into the tewat's yard and slid a grocery sack half-filled with mules' ear roots across the torn plastic seat of his pickup. He heard chanting from inside the house, quietly closed the pickup door, stepped onto the porch and listened. The unfamiliar song was sad and hopeful at the same time. When Raven Eye had finished singing, Isaac entered the house. Raven Eye lifted his head. "The Old Man is ready for us," he said with a smile.

The rocks were hot when the two men reached the sweat lodge, the water bucket already filled. They scooped the rocks to the center of the dome, then stepped outside to strip, one man wiry and wrinkled, the other a series of convex curves stacked into the spring air. They backed in and sat. Neither spoke as steam began to curl around their bodies. Isaac knew he would not follow his own path to Old Man today. This day belonged to a different old man, to his uncle, Raven Eye.

"Your grandmother came here often," Raven Eye finally began, "when your mother was at Carlisle." He paused as if reluctant to turn a page in a family album. "Your grandmother wouldn't take an allotment. She went back to Billy Moses after the railroad ran through her garden on the point below the mill site. That's when your mother was born." He ladled water onto the rocks. Fresh steam hissed between them.

Isaac wanted to probe, to pursue this footnote to the pages of his life, but he remained silent, giving himself to the steam and the heat and the voice he knew would return.

"We were the heathens, your grandmother and me, the evil ones the white spirit women spoke about," Raven Eye whispered. "We were together in the war." He ran the tip of his right index finger over the scar across his forehead. "We were there when your great grandmother Speaks-in-Tongues died at Big Hole. We were at Snake Creek when your great grandfather Two Crows was killed. I have waited for you for a long time."

Isaac heard the ladle rub against the edge of the cedar bucket, then the hiss of fresh steam as Raven Eye disappeared from view.

When the old man became visible, he spoke again, weighing his words like stones for the bottom of a fishnet. "A long, long time ago, our tewats knew that strangers would come from the east. Their dreams had told them. 'Our hearts will ache for five generations,' they said to the people." He sighed, then continued. "When the strangers did come, our people thought about killing them, but treating strangers unkindly was not our way. This is what I have been told, and what I have seen in dreams, and I know is true."

A faint sound began to circle Isaac as if the song Raven Eye had been singing earlier in the day was now traveling around the inside of the canvas walls of the sweat lodge. A journey song, Isaac reflected, as Raven Eye continued.

"When the strangers came, they had three chiefs. One was a war chief with a thin mouth and a strong voice. He showed our people a rifle that used no gunpowder, hard round water that could start a fire in seconds, and many other magical things. He frequently spoke of how powerful his people were. He talked more than he listened, and the people called him Grizzly Bear Robe Folded. The second chief was a medicine man with hair the color of warm coals. He listened more than he talked, frequently smoked a pipe, and the people called him Daytime Smoker. The third chief spoke with his hands and with his heart. He was one of us. He gave us a peace pipe with the head of a war axe, a sign of the white man's confusion. Later our tewats told us of things the people could not imagine—about brother against brother, of seeing our people's bones scattered across the earth, of being strangers in our own land. They were right in all these things. We are still in the belly of the monster."

Raven Eye sighed, dribbled water on the waiting stones, closed his eyes and began to rock back and forth.

Isaac wanted more, if only a thread or two tied together, a simple knot that one could grip in the mist that filled the small circle around them. He sucked in steam, held it like a hot spirit, slowly exhaled. He thought about searching for Old Man, couldn't wander from the scarred and wrinkled tewat sitting beside him, wasn't sure if there was always a difference. He, too, started to rock, slowly, rhythmically, his body a chant, the earth a drum.

"You are one of us." The old man's voice was steady now. "You come from the pipe, from the gift, from the promise that was broken. You can hear the voices. You are the fifth generation."

Isaac rocked farther forward with each beat, felt the floor of the sweat lodge rising towards him, touched warm earth with his forehead. He became lost in the voices murmuring like a mountain brook, gathering in pebbled pools, building courage and conviction. When he finally lifted his head and opened his eyes, the warm stones in the middle of the circle were his only companions.

Isaac slipped the dull brass key onto his pickup key ring, USPO stamped on one side, the slip in his pocket declaring that he could now be reached at P.O. Box 313. He had invested a five-dollar bill in this quiet hope, unwilling to rely on the grocery store grapevine to learn if his letter to Bernice would be answered. He had written to her the evening before, tree toads singing, the pungent smell of the river urging him on. He wrote about roots and Raven Eye, about the first salmon ceremony earlier in the week, about his plans to build a sweat lodge near the beach by the railroad bridge. He was going back, he wrote, while she was pushing forward. He hoped that her work was going well and hinted for an invitation.

He was spending increasing amounts of time with Raven Eye now. At first the old man's requests for various roots and stems and leaves had worried Isaac—ocean-spray for diarrhea, yarrow for fever, lupine for urination. While Raven Eye never seemed vigorous, Isaac did not think of him as ill. Then the requests broadened: Kinnikinnick for smoking, Oregon grape roots for dye. By early summer, bundles and baskets of plant life hung from newly driven nails and filled the walls and corners of Raven Eye's shack, the room now a magical blend of earthy scents. On each visit Isaac made, Raven Eye would review for him with story and song every plant and its uses—colds and fevers, pains and wounds, burns and snakebite—knowledge gleaned from thousands of years of living the landscape.

The river crested the first week of June, beached driftwood recording the high water mark. Syringa blossomed along the banks. Chinook gathered at the mouths of creeks, their rich flesh a cherished gift. Isaac gave his first few fish away, then roasted one on the strip of beach now reappearing near the railroad bridge. He dropped a large male by Doc Ryan's house, sold a few to the mill hands driving home from work with grease on their hands and sawdust in their hair. The town was tracking back to normal, with talk again of the price of wheat, rodeo stock and baseball scores.

At first Isaac read the flyers he pulled through the four-inch brass and glass door with 313 above the keyhole. Then, tired of the impersonality of *Postal Patron*, he missed a day, then two, and soon another week went by, and he started to feel like a ghost again, unnoticed and unwanted.

"Hi, Isaac." The clerk at the grocery store smiled as she rang up the non-iodized salt, the brown sugar and coffee, a jar of Skippy's peanut butter. "You got a postcard waiting for you. It came on Wednesday. Postmarked Pendleton."

"I'm not general delivery anymore," Isaac blurted, not sure of what else to say.

"I know," the clerk replied with a grin as she handed him his change. "The card is in your mailbox."

He crossed the street with his grocery sack, shifted it to his left arm as he passed through the post office door and took his keys out of his pocket. With his groceries at his feet, Box 313 opened with a click, and he pulled out a newsprint flyer and a single postcard. The name on the card was his, the box number correct, the handwriting familiar. The message on the back of the card contained only two words: *Keep trying.* The card was signed *Mom*.

Back on Main he looked again at the card, then repeatedly whispered those two words to himself as if memorizing them for a speech or play. When he reached his pickup he remembered the salt and sugar for brining his morning catch still on the floor in front of his mailbox. He retraced his steps, looked in Box 313 once more just in case, then retrieved his grocery sack. Through the post office door he saw a man carrying a large box attempting to push the door open with his shoulder and back. When Isaac opened the door to help, the man's body turned and directly above the top edge of the box was the face of Bill Sheffield. The two men exchanged stares. Their faces tightened. Isaac broke the stalemate, backed up three steps and let the pawnbroker pass. "Keep trying," he muttered to himself as he once more opened the door and stepped onto the street.

He wrote to Bernice again that night, light from his kerosene lamp shadowing his hand on the plain white stationery and the pencil with which he sketched the church on Tutuilla Road. He wanted to tell her he was full with spring, that he thought about her smile, her words, her shiny black hair, the small of her back, the curve of her hips, but he couldn't write what he said to himself in this quiet corner of his world. Instead he drew dried herbs hanging from a peeled log wall, a sweat lodge by the river's edge. He sketched his mother's Carlisle ledger book in one corner of the page, a pipe tomahawk in another. Then his pencil touched the empty space in the center of the page, and words appeared like a necklace of beads. "Climbing fast, no forks in the trail. I want to see you." He sketched a trillium for his signature, folded the letter, licked and addressed the envelope. His left hand trembled when he held the envelope just beyond the hot glass chimney and blew out the lamp.

The river had dropped another foot by the time Isaac started building his sweat lodge. For location he chose a patch of sand midway between his father's grave and his grandmother's garden site, the railroad bridge he'd walked so many nights linking these special places. He drew a circle seven feet across, punched an even number of holes into the waiting ground with a crowbar he'd found beside the road the week before. Willows came next, long and lithe, spring's yellow bark now lemon green. He sharpened the butt ends and stuck them into the circle of holes in the ground until he was completely caged. He bent the slender ends of two willows across the center of the circle and tied each to its opposite mate with binding twine he'd found at the edge of a nearby hayfield. Other willows joined the dome, twined together two by two, until a solid framework stood anchored to the earth. An outfitter's discarded wall tent provided a cover, one wall missing and a ceiling badly scorched. River stones secured the bottom of the canvas. He made a flap for the door and dug a shallow hole in the sand a few feet in front of the entrance for the fire pit. With more stones, strips of shredded cottonwood bark and several pieces of sun dried driftwood, his sweat lodge was ready.

A gibbous moon greeted him early that evening as he stepped from tie to tie above the river. Moonlight highlighted the dents in the stainless steel milk pail he carried and turned steel rails into beams of light shooting over the water. The fire caught easily. He placed more wood on fresh flames as if nudging a friend into conversation. When the rocks were ready he dipped his milk pail half full from the river, lifted some of the hot rocks to the center of the sweat lodge with a broken-handled shovel, eagerly stripped and backed in. Perhaps Old

Man would join him, he thought, as he wrapped himself in layers of heat and settled into a peaceful calm. Fresh steam soon filled his nostrils, and sweat dripped off the end of his nose. He was deliciously alone, yet connected to this narrow strip of sand and loam resting in the river's bend. He listened to the river eating at its outside banks, tumbling rough stones round and smooth. Cocooned, he dozed.

At first the beat of drums sounded distant, a resting heartbeat apart, then louder and more intense. A clear voice rose above the beat, high pitched and hopeful. Isaac recognized the song, a *Quilloowaya*, a woman's departure song for a man going on a dangerous journey. The song repeated two more times—a pleading, a prayer, a send off. When all sound had ceased, Isaac awoke with a start. He was slippery with sweat, his breathing was hard, and he felt the need to move, to walk or dance or run. A few steps took him to the river, to the eddy where the current turned back upon itself contemplating its next move. He waded in mid-thigh, leaned forward, splashed cold water on his face, his shoulders, his chest. His skin was smooth and clean, his mind clear. He backed again into the sweat lodge eager for the warmth, the afterglow, an opportunity to thank Old Man for his guidance.

The moon was mid-sky when he dressed, the sand surrounding the fire pit still warm on his bare feet. He emptied the milk pail and placed it back in the sweat lodge, then picked up the crowbar he had tucked under a driftwood log earlier that day. He felt its heft, nodded and walked quickly to the bridge.

Isaac was up early the next morning, a Friday payday at the local mill. He drove to town at noon, told Bobby he didn't need any green stamps when the young man filled his gas tank. He bought an extra quart of oil to have in his rig. At the hardware store he purchased a flashlight and a pair of leather gloves. He walked past the post office on his way back to his pickup, almost didn't stop, decided to empty Box 313 of its usual accumulation. A single envelope lay on the bottom of the box. It was addressed to Isaac Moses in a strong, attractive hand, Tutuilla Road part of the return. He slid the envelope under his shirt.

Bernice had gotten his letter. She wasn't sure what all the sketches meant, but she liked them, especially the trillium. She was waitressing half time. Truckers and cowboys didn't tip much, but she made enough without interfering with her real work. She didn't think gathering herbs was going to get much accomplished. She had noticed that the pipe in his drawing was a tomahawk as well, and that's the way it was with the whites—they thought they could buy peace and friendship with power.

Her last two sentences were what Isaac had waited for, what he had reached for dozens of times through the square glass door of his post office box with its gold numbers and brass hinges. *I waitress at Scotty's, east edge of town. I get off at 8:00 on Wednesdays and don't work Thursdays and Fridays.* A bold capital B served as the signature.

He read the letter again in his cabin, read it once more sitting on a pine log bench on his porch. Back inside, he removed a piece of paper and an envelope from a shelf by his bed and began to write. This time words made an easy appearance, wrapped line to line until they bumped into the bottom of the page, with just enough room for *Isaac* and a small trillium sketched in the lower right corner.

> *Dear Bernice,*
>
> *Your letter came today, a perfect day to hear from you. I have thought many times about my visit with you and my trip to Celilo. Many fish are here now, sharing themselves or swimming upstream to spawn.*
>
> *I told you about Raven Eye. Perhaps my mother has mentioned him too. I have learned much from him. Last evening I tried out my own sweat lodge. There is power in the fire, the steam and the rocks. Not everything is words and laws and treaties and committees. Some things can't be spoken.*
>
> *Tonight I am going away. I am not sure where or for how long, but as you told me on Tutuilla Road, even dreamers someday have to dance.*

He signed and folded the letter, addressed the envelope, found a stamp he had purchased just for this purpose. The space for the return address remained blank.

As shadows lengthened in the draw, Isaac brought out his clean pair of jeans, pulled the right front pocket inside out and cut off the pocket tip with his hunting knife. He packed his knapsack with this knife, his folding meat saw, three day's supply of elk jerky, and the gloves and flashlight he had purchased earlier in the day. He propped the crowbar he had carried from his sweat lodge beside his door and set the letter to Bernice on top of his pack. As his cabin fell dark, he sat on the bench beside his kitchen table and began to chant.

CHAPTER NINETEEN

1806

For half a moon Two Stars had listened to the joy in Spotted Fawn's voice as the two friends pushed their root digging sticks into moist earth or sat on the hillside overlooking their village. Spotted Fawn thought of nothing else now, only of her desire to be with the soyapo she had fallen in love with, the red-haired white man medicine chief who was gentle and kind. She had confided in Two Stars from the beginning—the walks up the canyon, the rides to the river, the scent of syringa, cedar and sex.

Two Stars had been more cautious with the strangers, had watched them from a distance, had avoided invitations. She'd been chosen by the spirits, her grandmother had told her, the only survivor of her family's lodge when the stinking death had killed her mother, her father and two older brothers. The pockmarks on her face reminded others of her calling. She had found her name on a mountaintop, the first star of the evening and the last star of the morning meeting in the middle of the night near where she stood. The voices that had guided her home still visited her on clear nights with an early moon.

Her people had known that strangers would come among them. "They will arrive from the east, men with big medicine and small hearts." That is what tewats had seen in their deepest dreams and described in winter councils. The strangers would come from another world, the tewats had declared, and would be difficult to understand. One more thing the tewats knew: following the strangers' visit, the people would have aching hearts for five generations.

But when the strangers' talking chief had finally smiled at Two Stars and signed his wish to meet her, caution fled. She had watched him run, the swiftest of them all. She had watched him talk to Nez Perce chiefs with his hands and eyes and had heard the words of agreement that followed. She had flirted and hid by the sandy beach across the river from the soyapos' camp. Twice he had met her there, the stranger with brown skin, hazel eyes and powerful arms.

The two young women schemed to delay in the valley when their village traveled to the tribe's spring gathering. It was Two Stars' time for the menstrual lodge, and Spotted Fawn would stay to bring her food and water and perhaps news of the strangers' camp on the north side of the river.

Two Stars didn't mind her monthly solitude. Twice a day her friend broke the quiet, jabbering like a bluejay.

The people of Broken Arm's village had departed, she told Two Stars. They had traveled up Camearp Creek to the prairie. Many of the bands were gathering there, from LaMota and Hasotin and Wallowa. They would talk about the soyapos and what the visit of these strangers foretold.

On the second day of Two Star's confinement, Spotted Fawn brought more news. The soyapos were collecting their horses and would leave the next day for Weippe. They would hunt there a few days and wait for the Nez Perce guides they had been promised. The snow would soon be crusted on the high ridges, grass tender on south-facing hillsides. When the time was right, Spotted Fawn's brother and cousin would guide the soyapos across the snowy mountains to the buffalo plains.

The news saddened Two Stars. She had hoped to meet the talking chief once more, to feel his strength by the river, to tell him she would wait for him if he chose to return after taking the white men home. She was surprised when Spotted Fawn announced her own intent to follow her brother to the mountains, to surprise the healing chief with her happy smile, to stay with him forever.

Two days later, the two women visited the soyapos' deserted camp. Three circles of blackened stone marked the ground near the ancient lodge ring where the strangers had kept their baggage. Their horse corral remained a jumble of criss-crossed poles and slanted posts driven hastily into the rocky soil. Two Stars looked for something to keep—a shell button or misplaced bead, some tangible piece of the strangers who had touched her young life. Spotted Fawn walked the camp head up, as if trying to catch a familiar scent rising from the gravel at her feet. Neither search proved successful, and that evening the two women returned to their nearly empty village. Stripped of their tule mat covers, the peeled pole frameworks of the longhouses looked like skeletons of large beasts standing upright between basalt bluffs on each side of the narrow canyon.

Six days passed slowly while Spotted Fawn waited for her brother. Two Stars helped her friend dig cous and pound the slim white roots into meal for bread. They made a hackamore from hemp gathered the previous fall. With each day of preparation, Spotted Fawn's determination grew. On the seventh day, her brother and cousin arrived at the village. Each had an extra horse, a blanket, and a bag of roots for their journey. The two women followed them to the river, watched them swim their horses across the swift current, then climb the hills to the north and east on the worn trail to Weippe. A short time later Spotted Fawn led her mare to the river and mounted. She kneed the pony into the crossing, her feet high on the mare's back as the two were swept downstream. Her right hand gripped the hackamore, her left the lower end of the horse's mane. She gave no backward glance as she followed her brother's trail through the deserted soyapo campsite and up the first ridge leading north.

Two Stars stood by the river immersed in the aching loneliness she had tried to ignore for the past ten days. Uncertainty pinned her in place. She had longed for one last night with her lover here beside the river, his hands speaking a truth she had not previously known. Now her best friend had left as well. She felt abandoned and alone. She listened to the river, looked for a sign, but earth and sky were silent.

Late afternoon she followed the riverbank upstream, crossed a low knob studded with pines and walked onto the horse-racing flat where she had watched her lover outrun all the young men from her village. She tried to hear the sounds again, the course breathing of the racers, the cheering of the crowd, but only an osprey called overhead. Back at the river, flotsam etched the sandy beach—pine bark and driftwood, feathers and fir cones in parallel lines defining the steps of the river's retreat. She paused near a small mound of ashes and remembered the warmth of the flames and the heat of her body as she and her lover rolled off his blanket onto the damp sand. She decided to spend the night here, to return to her village in the morning.

She bathed quickly in the chilly water, warmed herself in the day's last sunlight cutting through the deep notch the river had carved in the canyon. She had just finished dressing when she saw two riders at the edge of the shadow creeping up the valley's northern face. They were riding toward the river, pace strong, rifles slung over their shoulders.

Two Stars walked quickly to the river crossing and hid among the roots of an upturned cedar recently abandoned at the river's crest. The riders disappeared into timber, then emerged onto the flat along the river. They stopped at the former campsite, dismounted, and hobbled their horses. In the dusk she could not see their faces or the details of their clothing. She wanted desperately to believe that the talking chief was there, that he had come back to say goodbye or take her over the mountains.

Two Stars slipped through willows on her way back to the beach, shredding the inner bark from a dead cottonwood as she walked. She lifted a flat piece of cedar and a shaft of maple from her hemp-twined bag. A wisp of smoke soon rose from the hole in the cedar hearth, and fine hot powder trickled into the tinder. Her gentle breath coaxed the smoldering bark into flame.

Dry willow made a smokeless fire with a flickering light. The evening star appeared above the lumpy hills on the east side of the valley, a glowing dot in an otherwise empty sky. She fed the fire with four small branches and a lover's prayer. She knew both men would see the flame and hoped that one would understand its message.

CHAPTER TWENTY

1953

Isaac donned his pack and stepped off his porch exactly at midnight. Broken clouds moved up the valley, smearing dark patches across the moonlit landscape. He carried a crowbar like an abbreviated cane, curved end filling the inside of his fist, its chiseled tip dangling above the ground. He walked briskly down his lane, crossed the road, paralleled the river downstream. He was running on faith, on the blood in his veins, on the voices and the dreams.

At the north end of the railroad bridge he followed the tracks past the sawmill, security lights tracking the last vehicle from the swing shift departing the entrance gate. When the rails curved west, he stopped. Here the ancients had lived in their pit houses, Raven Eye had told him, and here Walking Woman had planted her beans and squash, had ditched water from a nearby creek, had been driven away by railroad men with shiny badges and white man papers. He imagined his grandmother planting seeds, pulling weeds, shucking beans in the shade of a nearby pine—the same gentle face and rhythmic motion he had seen in his cabin during his time of healing. His faint shadow dogged him back to the railroad bridge, its steel arches polished by moonlight. Counting the ties out of habit, he began to cross.

The back eddy on the far side of the river lay quiet. Striding east, he took two ties at a time. He left the rails at half a mile, pushed upslope through hackberry and hawthorn, paused under a prominent ponderosa at the edge of a patch of grass where marble and granite headstones kept vigil in the night. A scene emerged as Raven Eye had described it—the mule-drawn cart, his mother kneeling where he now stood, the scar on Raven Eye's forehead catching the morning light as he sang a departure song. Isaac walked to the third row south and paused in front of the stained marble stone marked James Girardoux, May 14, 1898 - December 10, 1918, Private, U.S. Army. His father was a soldier, Raven Eye had told him, who could never be killed by an enemy. He had died of the flu a week before his unit shipped to France. Isaac gave the headstone a respectful nod.

Alfalfa in the field on the far side of the road had gathered sufficient dew to dampen his pant legs as he waded through the tall stalks toward Highway 12. Three deer scattered to his left, jarring him momentarily off his pace. He soon returned to swinging the crowbar in his right hand past his damaged knee with a metronomic rhythm.

The highway was empty, and as he crossed the pavement his mind focused and vision narrowed. He skirted a streetlight and entered the alley just west of Main. At Fourth he checked his watch, felt his letter to Bernice against his chest, followed the alley one block south to the car lot behind the Texaco station. His pulse quickened as he leaned the crowbar against the chromed bumper of a '37 coupe, then undid the top two buttons of his shirt as he cut between the gas station and jewelry store to Main. Three stores north, he dropped his letter to Bernice into the slot on the top of the sidewalk mailbox. Its metal lid squeaked as he lowered it into place. The rest of Main lay calm as unsuspecting prey, shadows from street lamps lying on the pavement, pickups with their tool boxes and slip tanks parked beside the curb.

With his crowbar once more in hand and its swing matching his gate, he crossed Main. Beneath a street lamp his watch read 12:48, and a half block later he turned north. At the far end of the alley he set his pack on the lid of a battered garbage can, unbuckled the strap and retrieved his folding meat saw, then slid it in his left pants pocket beside his flashlight. Leather gloves were next, twisted together and stuffed under his belt. His pack fit neatly on top of the collection of cardboard and bottles beneath the garbage can lid. He tucked his hair beneath the collar of his jacket and pulled his cap bill low over his face.

The chisel end of the crowbar snagged momentarily at the hole he'd cut in the bottom of his right pants pocket, then glided along his thigh to below his knee with an unexpected chill. With the crowbar's crook lipped over the pocket's edge, he took a step, then two, adjusting his stride to a familiar limp. The click of hard steel against the copper rivet at the corner of his jeans pocket joined the sound of his breathing as he crossed Fourth. At exactly 1:00 a.m. he stepped over the curb and opened the side door to the Boots & Saddles Bar.

Smoke and laughter filled the path between the empty pool table and two huddles of patrons enjoying their last drinks of the night. Isaac walked straight to the men's room, ducked to avoid the 40-watt bulb hanging from the ceiling and quickly latched the door behind him. Everything in the rest of his plan depended on his understanding of the rhythm of a Friday night closing—customers pleading for one more drink, liquor laws begging the last ring of the till. His bladder felt full with the tension, and he decided to authenticate his wait. He had just finished peeing when he saw the barroom lights creep under the restroom door, heard familiar groans from the crowd and the shuffling of feet on the linoleum floor. He froze when the bathroom door rattled and shook inches from his face. The door latch held. An angry voice announced, "I'll piss in the goddam street," then faded into the quiet that gradually filled the familiar corners of this part of Isaac's former life. He switched off the light, listened to Cindy gather the empties and pick up the ashtrays, heard Jake announce that he'd sweep up in the morning. Isaac thought he heard the front door close, but wasn't sure. He pulled the crowbar up through the hole in his pants pocket, gently lowered the cracked oak toilet lid, straddled its oval form and sat. The smell of his own sweat partially masked the rankness of the nearby urinal. His breathing slowed and the waiting began.

With eyes closed, he mentally retraced his steps through the cemetery, wandered over the railroad bridge, visited the ancient pit house site where he had often played as a child. So much of him seemed buried in this strip of land split by a river, connected by a bridge, where voices shared a story he could not glue together, pages missing and paragraphs blurred. And now he sat on a toilet seat in a black pit of yellow stench mired between a past he could not understand and a future he could not create.

When he felt confident everyone had left the bar, he stood, groped his way to the bathroom sink and pulled a handful of towels from their metal dispenser. Recalling that the hot water faucet didn't work, he tried the cold, dribbled water on the towels and his sweaty hands. He could hear the beat of his heart as he stuffed the damp towels in the crack at the bottom of the door. He startled himself when he flipped on his flashlight, then shined the beam of light shoulder high to the left of the urinal and approached the familiar hole in the sheetrock. Peering inside, he could see the expected patchwork of red brick and gray mortar.

The beam from the flashlight jumped, and Isaac tried to calm himself with two long breaths. He propped the flashlight on the toilet lid, put on his gloves and took the folding meat saw from his pocket.

The sheetrock was easy, a horizontal cut left to a stud, then down its length to a foot above the floor. With even strokes he sawed to the right of the hole, waited for the blade to bite a second stud, smiled when he discovered the wall was built on 24-inch centers. He ran the blade in a quarter arc and began another vertical cut. Fine white dust drifted down the dirty wall with every backstroke until his saw caught and a jolting current jumped through his arm to his shoulder. His arm jerked back involuntarily. He smelled burnt metal and heard the clatter of the saw hitting the side of the toilet bowl. Shaking, he examined the saw blade with one tooth missing and three teeth blued. The beam of light still pointed in the right direction.

With sheetrock gone and copper wire noted, the real work began. The first brick was a challenge, mortar gradually yielding to the crowbar's tip, to thrusts, scrapes and grunts. He broke a second brick in half, crowbar wedged above it, curved end firm in his leather grip. Soon he was battering bricks oblivious of the noise, rivulets of sweat washing streaks through the mortar dust that covered his face. More bricks popped out with a single blow and a dull thud, twice requiring their hasty removal behind him. When the hole was half the size of a car door, Isaac took off his gloves, cupped his hands beneath the faucet and drank what he could while water dribbled down his shaking arms to the inside of his elbows. He pulled his watch from his pocket, said "2:09" out loud. Frenzy began to grip him as he sawed a hole in the sheetrock on the other side of the brick wall—above a pipe, below a wire—then worried the worn blade through two cuts of a white fir stud.

The sawed end of the stud protruding from the floor sill scratched his belly as he crawled over the water pipe near the bottom of the hole. The room before him was completely black, the vault door to the front part of the pawnshop tightly fitted to its threshold. As he stood he smelled the butt of a cigar, gun oil, a hint of brain-tanned buckskin. With dawn nearly an hour away, he was exactly where he wanted to be.

CHAPTER TWENTY-ONE

1806

A growing impatience pervaded the military encampment on the north side of the Kooskooskee. Trading trips to Pierced Nosed villages across the swollen river had slowed. Fresh roots and ropes, pack saddles and sleeping robes filled much of the circle of piled stones that formed the ancient pithouse walls at the center of the camp. Anxious mounts paced inside the pole corral on the grassy flat that bent the river west. In the morning the thirty-one men, one woman and a child would move their camp to Weippe to hunt and dry meat and wait for the guides the chiefs had promised. "Ten sleeps," Broken Arm had told them. Then Indian guides would lead the party east over rugged mountains to the buffalo plains, the last serious challenge between the Corps of Discovery and home. George Drouillard was the only member not eager to leave.

Drouillard didn't have a home, at least not a parcel of land surrounded by a fence or a house at the end of a graveled road. But his reluctance to leave this valley went far beyond that reality. During the four weeks of his stay, he had made friends here— Broken Arm, Red Grizzly Bear, Cut Nose and Twisted Hair. He had learned that the Nez Perce were a proud people in a rich land, generous and strong. And he had courted Two Stars, a woman with a calm spirit like his own and curves that wrapped around his body like warm, wet rawhide. For the first time on the entire expedition, uncertainty tugged at Drouillard. He was committed to the captains to complete the mission, but loath to leave in the morning.

That evening he slipped away from camp while Pierre Cruzatte fiddled and the men danced. He swam his horse across the river, skirted the willows upstream to a sandy beach, circled back to a cedar grove below the bend of the river. Disappointed, he made the three-mile ride up Camearp Creek to Broken Arm's nearly deserted village. Two old women signed Two Star's whereabouts to Drouillard—in a menstrual lodge where no man could go. Starlight guided him back to the river and the jubilant sounds of a Scottish jig.

During the Corps' four day stay at Weippe, Drouillard wandered from the camp when he could, preferring the company of fir and spruce to the restlessness of his human companions. A hard rain fell on the eve of their hasty departure, leaving the morning's route wet and slippery. They were backtracking now, guides forgotten, piecing together strips of trail sketched on maps and etched in their minds from the westward passing of the previous fall.

The first snow banks appeared the following day, filling hollows on north-faced slopes or lying in the bottoms of shaded cedar pockets. By afternoon crusted drifts claimed the trail in chunks—first one foot thick, then three, then five—sometimes bearing the horses' weight, sometimes engulfing them belly deep. That evening the men were quiet as they set up camp beside Hungry Creek. The captains, too, seemed caught in the grip of the creek's dark and lonesome canyon.

The query came mid-morning. The party had tried to ascend a side ridge leading to the mountains' highest backbone. Snow lay three feet deep beside the creek, six feet deep at mid-climb. Two miles farther, twelve feet of snow covered the slope, and the trail had vanished. As usual, it was Captain Clark who asked. As always, he requested certainty over probability.

Drouillard understood the warning these mountains had given them the previous fall. He knew that to proceed without Indian guides was folly. As the principal woodsman and guide of the group, he was asked a single question—could he follow the proper ridges of the mountains to make the crossing. Following a respectful pause, he stated that under the circumstances he had neither the knowledge nor the power to find the trail over these mountains.

During the two years of their journey, the Corps had never retreated. Drouillard watched as the captains walked a short distance from the group. They squinted into the harsh reflected light as they talked.

Their gesturing arms cut the crisp air. Their decision disappointed the men, yet was also a relief. All had read the signs—the dogtooth violets barely blooming on the Weippe, thick morning frost on Horsesteak Meadow, the lengthening sections of trail still wintered in. At the captains' order, they all slogged back to Hungry Creek. The broken snowpack through which they'd plodded now soaked their moccasins, chilled their legs and numbed their feet. As they halted for the night, a steady rain began.

"The cap'ns wanna see you," announced Francis LaBiche in French as he nodded in Drouillard's direction. The two men walked to the edge of a meadow where the captains and Charbonneau, his Shoshoni wife and their infant son were bivouacked among a cluster of giant spruce. The captains squatted beside the struggling campfire. LaBiche lingered in case interpretation would be needed.

Clark spoke to Drouillard in a determined voice. "You understand our situation," he began. "If we try the mountains and fail, we could lose everything—including our lives. If we don't cross these mountains soon, the Missouri will freeze before we can get back to St. Louis. That's it, plain and simple." He glanced toward LaBiche, who looked at Drouillard, who nodded his understanding.

"We must get guides," Clark continued. "You will leave in the morning."

Drouillard nodded again, this time directly at the captains.

"Offer a rifle," Clark continued, "to anyone who will lead us to Traveller's Rest."

The Shoshoni woman fed dead spruce limbs into the fire, which momentarily splashed the men's faces with light. Lewis cleared his throat. "If you have to," he added, "offer two rifles, and add ten horses if someone will take us to the Great Falls." Drouillard waited for any additional instructions, stood, repeated in sign and broken English what he was to do. LaBiche said "oui," and the captains nodded in assent.

"Take someone with you," Clark directed, "and take the short cut back to the river."

Drouillard and George Shannon left camp beneath the morning star, riding carefully through the dark timber along Hungry Creek. By noon they had backtracked to the ridge where slabs of granite pushed through the forest floor. They stopped to chew on camas bread while their horses fed on short fresh grass at the edge of a melting snowbank.

Descending the ridge to Collins Creek, Drouillard considered trail time as he rode, adding an hour for slippery ground, subtracting two for the lightness of their load. If they pushed their horses hard enough they could cross the river the middle of the next day. His mind kept halting at the riverbank and circling the sandy beach upstream from the crossing. They slackened their pace. At the first meadow on Collins Creek their horses fed two hours before dusk.

Late the next day the two men paused at the top of the ridge above the river, the south-facing slope a carpet of green falling in folds to the valley floor. In open country now, they slung their rifles over their shoulders and rode toward the shade gradually rising to meet them.

Their horses chomped an occasional clump of grass on the trail to the ancient lodge ring that had been the center of their camp for nearly a month. Horses hobbled, the two men separated in search of firewood. Shannon walked toward the patch of pine on the downstream point; Drouillard checked the riverbank for any fresh deposits of driftwood. He listened to the water as the evening star appeared like a cautious doe at the edge of a meadow. He lived by sign—the pad of a bear on a damp creek bank, a hoof print on a dusty rock. But the signs that spoke most clearly to him came from the sky, from the eagles, hawks and ravens, from the curve of a crescent moon or the light of an evening star. He gathered an armload of cedar drift from a level line near the shore and slowly returned to camp. He was retrieving his flint and steel from his possibles bag when he saw a flicker of light at the edge of the beach a quarter mile upstream. The flicker grew into a steady flame.

Drouillard had mounted his horse by the time Shannon returned. They agreed to meet in the morning at the mouth of the creek a mile below Broken Arm's village. Drouillard rode quickly to the top of the river crossing and urged his horse into the current.

On the south side of the river he rode east on the racing flat, then tethered his horse beside a hawthorn. With an evening breeze in his face, he approached the fire. At 60 feet he could see Two Stars' shoulder, the side of her face. She was alone, staring downstream toward the campfire now blazing boldly on the other side of the river. He had known he would find her the morning he left Hungery Creek, but he hadn't realized how beautiful she would be waiting for him in the firelight. He spoke her name softly. She turned toward him and smiled.

When Drouillard sat beside her, neither spoke. Two Stars added dry willow to the flames, and yellow light danced on their hands, arms and faces. They clung to each other, fumbled their way through clothing, fell together onto the moist sand at the edge of the river rushing past them.

Drouillard woke before dawn to gentle breathing at his side. He brushed away strands of hair that covered Two Stars' face, slid off her jaw and draped over a strip of otter fur lying on the sand. The circular scars that covered her cheeks and chin erased the indecision he had struggled with for the past two weeks. He slid from under the squirrel hide robe that covered them, moved quickly to the edge of the sandbar and waded into the chilling water. He bathed quickly, confident in his decision.

Two Stars sat up while he was dressing, shivered, wrapped her robe around her. Drouillard sat beside her. With his thumb extended from his fist, he touched the center of his chest. He slid four fingers over his heart, then moved his open hand back and forth a few inches from his chest, telling Two Stars that he had an aching heart. She extended her palm from her mouth, then moved her hand quickly toward her lips, asking him to talk.

He drew his open right hand across his forehead just above his eyes, giving the sign for *white man*, then followed with the sign for *many*. He pointed toward the east and twice repeated the sign for *white man.* Two Stars nodded that she understood. He again gave the sign for *white man*, followed by *heart* and *good*, then *heart* and *bad.* Two Stars signed both *know* and *no*, indicating that she did not understand, and repeated *talk to me.*

Drouillard realized the difficulty of his task, the contradiction in his message and even in his life. He was a half-breed, a witness at the jagged edge of two Americas. He glanced at his possibles bag tucked beneath a drift log, at his powder horn and shot pouch nearby. Then he noticed the pipe tomahawk he had propped against a willow by the side of their makeshift bed. He picked it up and sat on the sand within arm's reach of Two Stars. He again made the sign for *white man*, pretended to smoke the pipe tomahawk, then swung it up and down as if striking someone. He put the pipe tomahawk on the blanket between them, then repeated the sign for *white man* and signed both *war* and *peace.* Two Stars signed that she understood.

He made the sign for *time in the future*, pointed to Two Stars, and signed *woman* and *medicine.* Two Stars smiled. He again pointed toward Two Stars, then held his hand palm up in front of his lips and moved his hand forward several times. He signed quickly now, wanting to rid himself of the burden he had carried the past few weeks. He once more made the sign for *white man*, then placed his left hand flat in front of his chest, palm down, slid his right hand underneath the palm with index finger extended, crooked the finger and drew it quickly away. Finally he pushed both of his hands toward the ground and spread them sideways away from his body. Once again he signed that she must tell the people, then repeated the message: *the white man will take your land.*

Two Stars' smile had disappeared before he had repeated the message. She drew her robe tightly around her shoulders, extended her arms enough to give the sign for *question.* She pointed to Drouillard and extended her two index fingers side by side in front of her in the sign for marriage.

Drouillard's body stiffened. A mourning dove cooed to its mate against a background of water pouring swiftly over cobble. He picked up the pipe tomahawk and offered it to Two Stars. When she took it gently from his hands, he pointed once more toward the center of his chest, then followed the sign for *heart* with that for *know.* He moved his open right hand past his right ear and repeated this motion four times, telling Two Stars he would remember her forever. They both understood his message.

CHAPTER TWENTY-TWO

1953

Isaac scanned the inside of the walk-in vault of Uncle Bill's Pawnshop in the weakening beam of his flashlight. The black vault door stood on his left, the glimmer from its worn brass handle a compass point in his search. Rifles and shotguns were racked against the north wall. A mission oak library table with a single chair stood in the middle of the room. He turned clockwise with the light across an assortment of cabinets and bookcases, cluttered shelves and a chifforobe. A rolltop desk appeared, a bentwood chair parked askew near one end, twin milk glass lamps with Lincoln drapes perched above the S-curve roll. He took four quick steps, eagerly slid the rolltop open, then moved the light past cubbyholes stuffed with pawn tickets and envelopes, stamps and pencils and three cigars. The desktop itself was littered with paper, a stapler, a Zippo lighter, a dirty ashtray. The drawers offered little more —paper files and magazines, old calendars, note cards and two unopened bottles of scotch.

He passed the library table, the top bare, a pile of *Old West* magazines on the shelf below. A map cabinet against the east wall was next, rows of three-inch drawers stacked four feet high. Three gracefully tapered pestles leaned against the front of the cabinet. The top drawer opened easily. Isaac tapped the flashlight against his thigh, shined its beam across a map with *Captain Mullan* in the title, slid the drawer closed. Five more drawers yielded similar results. Shaking his head, he moved quickly to the lawyer's bookcase three feet away, the oak-trimmed glass doors framing the rows of hardbacks filling the shelves. He slid the top door open, noticed the space between the books and the back of the case, pulled several books forward onto the floor and cast the flashlight's beam into the dark corners. The other shelves followed, his left arm sweeping each in turn, books landing in a jumble on the oiled fir floor.

His impatience grew stronger, his flashlight weaker. He moved to his left, where cases of arrowheads were stacked in a painted pie safe he hadn't noticed in his first sweep of the room. The chifforobe was his last hope. In the wardrobe section he found a buckskin dress, elk ivories and brass thimbles dangling beneath a row of dentalium shells that paralleled the neckline. Behind the dress an empty parfleche leaned into a corner. A woman's woven cedar hat rested nearby. The flashlight flickered. Isaac banged it against the side of the chifforobe, and the light went out.

He could hear his heart pounding in his head, and he gulped stale air as if drowning in the blackness. He felt caught, a coyote in a #3 Newhouse waiting for the trapper to arrive. For the first time since he had left his house at midnight he doubted the outcome of the night, dawn less than an hour away. The odor of a stale cigar filtered out of the dark, and he stepped cautiously forward until the edge of the rolltop desk bumped his thigh. He patted the cluttered desktop until his left palm hit the ashtray, then brought his right hand down to where he knew the Zippo stood. The top of the lighter clicked as he opened it. His thumb stroked the igniter and a yellow flame leaped into the air. With his left hand he lifted a kerosene lamp from the top of the desk and placed it on the desktop, then carefully removed the sooted chimney. The wick was wet and readily grabbed the flame. He snapped the Zippo shut and slid it into his pocket, replaced the chimney and adjusted the wick. The room glowed in yellow light.

Cradling the lamp in both hands, Isaac returned to the chifforobe and set the lamp in front of the oval mirror above the drawers. Sheetrock dust smudged the nose and forehead of the face the mirror reflected and a red welt crossed the right cheek like war paint. Desperation sharpened the corners of both eyes.

A cornhusk bag filled the shallow depth of the top drawer, geometric patterns muted in the lamplight. The second drawer held moccasins paired in place, a collage of quill and beadwork. The bottom drawer was empty.

He fought looking at his watch, carried the lamp to the center of the vault, visually circled the room to the edge of light that surrounded him. Panic began to spread across his chest. He wanted to scream, to flee, to finish the task of tearing this place apart. He walked slowly toward the guns, then noticed again the row of pestles standing like sentinels in front of the lower drawers of the map cabinet, their graceful curves worn smooth by generations of his ancestor's hands. He set the lamp on the right front corner of the cabinet to catch as much light as possible down its face, knelt, swept aside the heavy pestles with both arms and opened the third drawer from the floor. Three bone quirts lay top-side up, braided horsehair winding across the checkered shelf paper that lined the bottom of the drawer. He slid the drawer closed, took a deep breath, and opened the one immediately below. At first the drawer appeared empty, but in the left back corner laid a small, thin book, pocket size and unassuming. With the ledger book in the light, he recognized the worn threads of the plain tan cover, opened the first page to be sure, then slid the book down the inside front of his denim shirt. His right leg began to cramp, but he reached for the porcelain knob of the bottom drawer and jerked it to its backside catch. A buckskin bag slid into view. He picked it up, felt the weight of its contents, undid the tie at the top of the bag and slid the worn buckskin down a wooden shaft. The end of the shaft joined the bowl and blade of a pipe tomahawk head, pewter gray in the shadow. Gripping the bag, he tried to stand. His right knee buckled, and he grabbed for the front of the cabinet.

Only clocks keep measured time, dividing equally the days, months and years of one's existence. Just before a late spring dawn the earth can pause, can almost stop before the light arrives and the warmth begins. Isaac felt the cabinet shake, watched the Lincoln-drape lamp tip slowly like the hand of a clock past one, chimney at two, faster to three. The thin glass reached five just before hitting the stone pestles piled at the base of the cabinet. Shards of milk glass and wisps of chimney expanded into space. Greedy flames chased kerosene across the oiled floor.

Holding the pipe bag, he skirted the lines of fire, crawled over sheetrock, pulled his chest and belly and thighs over the rough edges of sawed off studs. The bent point of a 16-penny nail snagged the back of his hand, and he ripped the hand free. He groped his way past the urinal, fumbled with the latch on the bathroom door, tore it loose with a shoulder lunge that left the door dangling from a single hinge. The heavy edge of the pool table in the main room of the Boots and Saddles Bar corrected his path to the bar's side door. He punched the lock in the center of the doorknob as he stepped onto the sidewalk.

The town lay still. Stars had disappeared from the northeast sky. Fighting the urge to run, he crossed Fourth and pulled his backpack out of the trash can, then re-crossed the street and continued down the alley past the brick wall at the back of the pawnshop. The night light at the Chevron station looked more forgiving than the street lamp, so he cut through the gas pumps, checked the highway, walked quickly to the hayfield on the other side. He was racing the dawn now, a light shadow lurking to his left.

He slowed when he gained the thornbush thicket, renewed his pace on the railroad tracks behind Cemetery Hill. Daylight found him stepping from the last tie on the railroad bridge on the north side of the river. He was hidden in cottonwood cover when the first siren wailed the town awake. A police car added its shrill whine as Isaac reached his Ford in the driveway, popped the door and slid behind the wheel. He sucked in a long breath, pulled the choke and pumped the pedal twice. The motor caught.

He could feel the ledger book against his left side at the bottom of his ribs. Beside him lay the pipe tomahawk in its buckskin bag. The engine smoothed. Isaac dropped the gearshift into second and eased the rig onto the gravel road. Across the river a giant torch chased away the last of the night sky.

CHAPTER TWENTY-THREE

1953

The first truck of the day pulled into Cory's Mill as Isaac passed, big pine, eight logs to the load. He turned right at the Odd Fellows Hall—too late for bar traffic, too early for the coffee crowd, but not willing to risk being seen on Kooskia's Main Street. Only two house lights were on in the six blocks of Front Street that defined the length of the town, and he soon cornered a row of junked out cars inside the curve that returned him to the highway on the south side of town.

Across the Southfork bridge the sun had found the copper hood of the steeple over the Presbyterian Church. Isaac slowed, then stopped. He undid two buttons of his torn shirt and retrieved the ledger book nestled above his belt, then wrapped the book in a T-shirt lying on his pickup seat and laid it in a corner of his pack. Three hundred yards ahead, smoke lifted through the cottonwoods in the vicinity of Raven Eye's sweat lodge. A short drive later Isaac turned onto the gravel weed patch that surrounded the tewat's house, then braked the Ford to a gentle stop. He opened the house door as quietly as he could.

A weak voice greeted him. "I thought you'd be here soon."

"Did you expect me this early?" Isaac asked, puzzled.

"I started a fire nearly an hour ago," Raven Eye replied.

Isaac paused, wanting to tell the old man about the fire in the pawnshop and what he had found. Raven Eye rocked slightly forward. Isaac sat.

"I had a dream," the old man began, closing his eyes. "Two rivers traveled through deep canyons and dark nights. Each finally took a new path and they flowed together. Many salmon swam up the new river, and life was good for the people." He turned his face in Isaac's direction and opened his good eye. "What do you think this means?"

Isaac hesitated, then with the fingers of his right hand stroked the pipe bag on the floor beside him. He pulled the pipe tomahawk slowly from its case.

"Maybe this is part of your dream." He moved closer, picked up Raven Eye's hand and placed the tomahawk's head in the old man's palm. Raven Eye looked straight ahead. His fingers circled the rim of the pipe bowl, followed the front of the head to the bottom of the blade. Thumb and index finger curved along both sides of the cutting edge from toe to heel. They stopped on a nick at the back of the blade, carefully explored this worn chip in the metal. Finally, Raven Eye stroked the shaft with his right hand, fingers stopping on a narrow groove in the shaft just above the grip. He grunted an *uh-huh*, and a wide smile filled his wrinkled face.

"Feel in the bottom of the bag," he directed Isaac.

Isaac's broad palm stretched the bag's drawstring top. He pushed his arm in past the elbow until his fingertips touched a flattened seam, then followed the seam to the left corner of the bag.

"Feels like maybe a bead down there, deep in the corner," Isaac stated matter-of-factly.

"Roll it out," Raven Eye directed.

Isaac held one corner of the bottom of the bag and sloped the soft hide toward his cupped hand. A single bead rolled onto his palm. "A blue bead," he told Raven Eye.

The old man began to sing, his voice thin, brief pauses punctuated by labored breath. Isaac did not recognize the song, a circle of paths and words, a coming together, a going home. Raven Eye completed the song a single time and stopped. "The stones are ready," he said softly. "It's time to go." He stood, steadied himself and walked to the door.

White stones in orange-red coals greeted them at the end of the familiar path, along with a blue enameled lidless coffee pot with two tin cups.

Isaac completed the preparations for their sweat—hot rocks scooped inside the sweat lodge, cedar bucket half filled from the river, bark mats laid in place. At Raven Eye's request he also filled the pot half full and placed it near the coals. The two men disrobed. Summer air licked their bodies as they backed into the sweat lodge.

For several minutes they sat in silence. Isaac imagined he could hear the old man thinking, like pebbles in a mountain brook tumbling downstream after a heavy rain. His arms and shoulders began to ache, and he noticed blood seeping between his fingers from the tear in his hand now warmed in the thickening steam. Scenes from the previous few hours of his life appeared collage-like in front of him, and then his mind began to clear.

"We are all coyotes on the land," Raven Eye began. "We come and we go and are here forever."

The old man ladled a cup of water onto the waiting stones, let the hiss slowly disappear and continued.

"My mother told me this story, how it was when the first soyapos were here. Her grandmother was born near Tsemenicum five years before the smallpox traveled upstream from Celilo and killed whole villages. The disease left her face pocked with scars the size of jack pine seeds. Two Stars was her name. She had powerful medicine even as a child. When the soyapos stayed in the valley waiting for the mountain snows to melt, Two Stars caught the eye of one of their men. She had a child the following spring."

Isaac drifted in the steam, mentally trying to follow the links from grandmother to grandmother. He could hear Raven Eye's breathing, slow and uncertain.

"Did your mother tell you about her grandfather?" Isaac asked.

Raven Eye swayed forward, became partly visible for a moment, then disappeared back into the mist. Isaac knew he could not ask the question again. He waited.

“He was a man of much power,” Raven Eye stated after a lengthy silence. “He was a fast runner and had a good heart.” Raven Eye inhaled a long stream of hot air and let it out slowly. “He came back to see Two Stars after the soyapos had left for the mountains. He gave her the pipe, the pipe you have now, and told her the white man would steal our land.”

Isaac slowly glued together the old man’s words. He remembered the voices by the railroad tracks, the men racing on the flat above the river, the shouts and laughter. He imagined the men running, the crowd cheering, Two Stars watching.

“We should bathe in the river now,” Raven Eye said, “and then we’ll have some tea.”

Sunlight sparkled on ripples and bounced off pools. Raven Eye used a walking stick as they waded thigh deep in the current, rinsed salt and sweat from chest and belly, splashed their faces fresh. Back at the sweat lodge, Raven Eye took a small bag of dried leaves from his sweatpants pocket and sprinkled some in each blue cup. He filled the cups with hot water from the enameled pot. While the tea steeped, he sang another journey song. Isaac joined in on the third round. They squatted by the few stones still in the fire pit, sun warming their backs and shoulders, and slurped their tea from the hot rim of the metal cups. Taking the last of the hot stones with them, they reentered the lodge.

“It was a long, long time ago,” Raven Eye began when the sweat lodge was once more filled with steam, “when the two-leggeds first came to this land. A great bear met a boy here in the valley. The bear was angry with this newcomer for invading its territory. The animal snarled his lips and chomped his teeth and decided to kill the two-legged. It growled so loudly the mountains shook, but the boy stood his ground. 'I can only die,' he told the bear. 'I am not afraid.'"

Astonished at the young boy's bravery, the bear decided to share his knowledge with the youth, to show him the plants and animals the two-leggeds could use for food, clothing and shelter. The bear put the boy on its back and carried him over jagged ridges, across slopes thick with beargrass, past stacks of stones ten men tall to buffalo country. Then the old grizzly brought the boy back to the hills overlooking Kamiah. 'Go tell your people what you have learned,' the bear told the boy, and then it disappeared."

Isaac was sweating profusely by the time Raven Eye finished his story. The old man lifted the flap to the sweat lodge and motioned for Isaac to follow.

This time they did not go to the river. Instead, Raven Eye reached again into the pocket of his gray sweatpants heaped near the entrance and pulled out two slender stems of willow. The sticks were peeled and slightly curved. He handed one to Isaac, and the two men walked downstream to a patch of grass at the end of the pebble beach. "We must get ready," Raven Eye said. He turned partially away and slid the willow down his throat. He bent forward as he brought the stick back out, and a stream of bile flowed evenly from his mouth and blended into the fresh grass.

Isaac knew what was expected of him. He gagged with the first insertion and pulled the willow out too quickly. He thought about how easy the old man made this seem, how practiced were his rituals, his stories and songs. Determined, Isaac ran the willow deep, chased it out with bitter tea and the tension of his night's work. He felt suddenly calm, stepped to the river, dipped his cupped hands into the water and raised what he could to his lips. When he glanced up the shallow bank, Raven Eye was returning to the sweat lodge.

"It is time for you to listen to Old Man," Raven Eye proclaimed when both had sat again on their cedar mats and fresh steam had filled the space between them. His arm shook slightly as he ladled more water onto the hot rocks.

For a moment Isaac wondered if buildings were still burning, if the fire had spread, but his stomach was calm and his body felt light. He began to think about his mother, his grandmother, about Carlisle and Oklahoma, about his own exile from his people and from the land. He tried to clear his mind, to ignore the old man sitting across from him asleep or in a trance, this withered bundle of wisdom he had grown to love.

He waited. No voices spoke. No images appeared. He thought about Two Stars, about Drouillard returning from the mountains, about the boy and the bear climbing the hogback to the sky.

Raven Eye lifted his gnarled chin from a sunken chest. His voice seemed to come from far away. "You must go quickly," he said to Isaac. "Follow your people, and you will know what to do."

CHAPTER TWENTY-FOUR

1953

Kooskia yawned as Isaac drove north on Main, a morning pause between loggers with their headlights on and storekeepers arriving with sufficient confidence or hope to get them through another day. Isaac had neither confidence nor hope but instead a calm confusion—his body relaxed from the heat of the sweat lodge, his mind trying to sort the details of the last six hours of his life. He stared down the middle of the street as if not seeing anyone was the same as not being seen. His first decision was easy. The road past Corey's Mill returned to Kamiah, a branch to the right led to Boller's Bridge and the Bitterroots. He made a right hand turn.

Across the river a gravel road climbed Kidder Ridge, requiring second gear on the frequent curves. Near the top, he pulled out on a point on the left side of the road and rolled down his window for a clearer view. To the west, a gray haze rose above the hills surrounding

Kamiah. Back on gravel, he increased his speed and soon topped out near the Kidder schoolhouse with double sash windows and clapboard siding clinging to its fieldstone foundation. Confusion lingered, the calm did not.

An hour later the Ford stopped as if of its own accord, and Isaac stepped onto the side of the road. He stretched and peed, then walked to a clump of nearby fir and sat on a fallen log. Musselshell Meadows spread before him a half-mile wide. Camas seedpods clung to their spindly stems amongst the thick grass. He scanned the open flat, studied the hidden corners along the meadow's timbered edge. Soon images of elk-hide tipis began to appear, three here, four there, until more than a hundred lodges completed a series of circles on the far side of the creek. Horses were next, two thousand strong, grazing belly deep in fescue. Isaac searched for the people—children playing, women digging camas and baking bulbs, young boys herding horses, warriors circling the perimeter—but the camp was empty.

"Follow your people," Raven Eye had whispered just two hours earlier. Here on this meadow the bands of White Bird and Looking Glass, Toolhoolhootzote and Joseph had readied themselves for their mountain escape. When Raven Eye's words came together, Isaac began humming a journey song. By the last verse the meadow was alive with people gathering ponies, taking down tipis, hanging parfleches and baskets of camas from the high pommels of rawhide saddles. Isaac knew he must follow.

He drove to Beaver Dam Saddle, the dirt road wet from recent snowmelt. Narrow wedges of crusted drifts slowed progress as he crossed the ancient route over Rocky Ridge. Weitas Meadows was melted out and thick with fawn lilies and mosquitoes. He could feel the people here, grass and water inviting their stay, thin columns of smoke from their campfires merging above the tops of giant hemlocks.

The tongues of snow across the road grew wider as he climbed out of Deep Saddle, the right side of the Ford bouncing over their hard packed surfaces, the left side flirting with the narrow road's outside shoulder. An urgency gripped him now, as if some intersection of time and space required his presence. On an inside curve in a hemlock grove on the north side of Willow Ridge he shifted into first, gunned the engine and climbed a sloping drift with all four wheels. The pickup busted through the crust, and both axles sank in course-grained snow. Isaac sat, anchored to the truck and the road and the mountain. For the first time since Musselshell he wondered what to do. He was stuck, or rather, he concluded, his pickup was stuck. The adrenaline that had kept him going for the past twelve hours slowed, and hunger and exhaustion competed for his attention. He had almost finished a piece of jerky when he let himself slide sideways across the pickup's seat and rested his head on his pack to sleep.

Two hours later he awoke with a crook in his neck and a dull ache in his cramped right knee. He sat up, rolled his head twice in a left hand circle, then repeated the same move clockwise. With sleep had come a reassurance about his route. He was fleeing Kamiah, just as his ancestors had done, following his people as Raven Eye had advised. A higher part of the mountain lay ahead. He stepped out of the cab, hefted his pack and began a rhythmical pace that adjusted itself to the steep climb to Liz Butte Saddle, then the downhill slope to Noseeum Meadows and the sidling trail along the hogback leading east.

By late afternoon his pace slowed, his right knee arguing the case for rest. At the highest point of a mile-long ridge, Isaac stopped. Mountain peaks defined a sawtooth horizon in all directions, a giant circle of ancient rock a hundred miles across, like a grand-scale upthrust medicine wheel with Isaac at its center. Beside him rose a granite cairn laid stone on stone by ancestral hands to mark this sacred place. He fingered the braid of sweet grass which Raven Eye had given him, remembered the Zippo lighter he had slipped into his pocket much earlier in the day. A waning thermal carried smoke and message skyward. He began to sing.

When his prayer for guidance had ended, he looked east toward a column of stones poking thirty feet into the graying sky, each stone larger than ten men could lift. He snuffed the sweet grass and started walking, passed a second stack of weathered rock, then a third and fourth. The columns led him into a pocket of jack pine. Emerging on the other side, Isaac stared, then froze.

From the top of the nearby ridge, a granite beast stared back with a three-foot eye in the side of its reptilian head. Its torso stretched six times the length of that head, and segments of tail trailed east for sixty yards. Here at the top of a wind-swept ridge in the center of a circle of mountain peaks all weakness had weathered away, leaving a palpable, humbling power. This was the hole in the sky that Raven Eye had once described, where prayers could more easily find their natural path. Isaac stood for a long time in the last sunlight of the day filtered through slender pines in narrow slices. The mountain air began to cool and settle down the craggy slopes below him, though this was not the cause of the shiver that traveled the length of his body before he moved again.

The creature's head rested on four large rocks protruding from the earth beneath its lower jaw. Isaac approached the head, then walked beside the high-arched back and stepped from segment to segment of the jagged tail that defined the serrated ridgeline. He could feel the energy that flowed between the curves of granite carved by a million years of spring rain and winter wind, freeing the spirit inside this piece of the mountain's ragged crust.

A light rain began to fall. He retraced his last few steps, his legs now heavy weights, his own energy seeping into the granitic soil beneath him. By the time he reached the head of the beast he could barely walk. He took off his pack, studied the four rocks holding the head four feet above the ground, then crawled into the cave-like space beneath its chin and sat. Soon his eyes closed, his arms fell limp into his lap and he rolled onto his left side. The evening shower slackened, then quit. Occasionally, Isaac's right cheek twitched and his bad leg stretched and curled. The conscious part of the longest day of his life had ended.

Well before dawn, the dream began. "I wanted you to see the falls before they're gone." Isaac saw a small gold cross on a white blouse above a gray wool jumper. Long socks covered the girl's legs above polished leather shoes. She extended her left hand toward him, palm up, holding a canvas-covered ledger book catching moonlight through the trees. "Someone must tell the story," the girl continued, then disappeared into the shadow on the dark side of the stony beast.

When Isaac's breathing had slowed, the rise and fall of his chest indiscernible in the black hole in which he slept, his grandmother appeared standing by her garden on the flat by the railroad bridge as sweating gandydancers buried her corn and carrots with creosoted ties and shiny rails. Next, orange columns of brilliant flames chewed into a mountain dawn amid the acrid smell of burning hides and rifle powder. Then a young man crawled on horse-trampled earth holding the right side of his face. Blood dripped down his arm and gathered in the inside crook of his elbow. A wailing girl slashed her hair and wrist with a jagged curve of broken glass. A wolf howled, and a woman clutched a black book to her chest and cried. Scenes kept rushing through Isaac's mind like a late spring flood —ripping at the riverbank, rolling rock and muck along the bed, choking everything in its path. Isaac's lungs ached, his arms flailed, and he began to drown in his own dream. When he tried to stand, he slammed the back of his head against the slab of rock above him. He fell to his knees, tried to shake the foggy blur out of his head, then sat.

Out of that fog, they emerged—a ragtag bunch with a steady pace, a moving museum of possibles bags and powder horns, rifles, blankets and pipe tomahawks. Two Nez Perce men held the lead, followed closely by a red-haired man on an elegant gray gelding. Twice the man glanced back at the band behind. A Shoshoni woman rode mid-group, her child asleep in a cradleboard tied on the side of her mottled mare. A yew wood sprig dangled from the willow arc over the child's head and bobbed each time one of the mare's hooves met ground. Isaac could hear the horses blow, the men's small talk and an occasional curse. Most men led a pack horse lightly loaded. The riders looked straight ahead as they passed.

Isaac shook his head again trying to bring edges into focus. A crisp movement in the jack pine swale below him grabbed his attention. Something was coming toward him, swiftly, silently, with a powerful ease. He could see a red bandanna stretched across a broad forehead. Leather fringe swayed from the shoulders of the man's elk skin shirt. Course black hair brushed cheekbones high set in a weathered face. The man drew closer. His Kentucky rifle moved rhythmically with each step. The bone handle of a sheath knife protruded from the left side of the linen sash around the man's waist. With a few long strides he was on the trail. When he came abreast of the granite beast, the stranger stopped. His eyes tracked the top of the creature's head, the shoulders, the back, the tail. His focus returned to the creature's hollowed eye, then dropped directly to the sheltered nook where Isaac sat. Their eyes locked briefly as the morning star broke the backbone of the Bitterroots.

When Isaac stirred, sunshine gilded the trail before him. A nutcracker flew past, its black tail outlined with the bright white of its belly. A morning breeze shared a hint of mountain heather. A squirrel on a nearby pine limb scolded Isaac for his presence.

Isaac sat, remembered the four rocks that held up the roof of his makeshift cave, glanced quickly at each for reassurance, returned to the easy slump of his shoulders and the calm beating of his heart. He crawled into open air and stretched his full frame into the morning. He surveyed once more the wind-carved granite bellied against the ridgetop.

The ground on which he stood was damp from rain. Recalling part of his dream, he turned toward the trail, took five swift strides to its edge and roved its surface with an inquisitive gaze. A single set of tracks marked the concave course. The prints lay crisp and huge. Sometime before dawn a grizzly bear had tracked through the jack pine walking the ancient trail. The bear had paused near where Isaac slept, had stood on its hind legs, dropped front feet to the damp ground and turned, then set a steady pace back in the direction from which it had come.

Isaac gathered his pack and backtracked west.

CHAPTER TWENTY-FIVE

1953

Following the tracks of the grizzly on the hogback trail, Isaac left behind the visions and the voices at the hole in the sky in the center of a circle of mountains. The bear had set a strong pace along the wind-swept ridge to Noseeum Meadows, then abandoned the trail near Sherman Peak and headed for the Weitas drainage. Isaac wanted to follow, to ride that bear home, to gather leaves, roots and stories and share them with all who needed to heal and understand, but a new reality stalked him as he walked the three remaining miles to his pickup. Thoughts of burning buildings narrowed his wishes to a single desire to flee. For half an hour he rammed his shovel into the compacted snow beneath the rear axle and transfer case of his pickup, then backed the two miles of twisted road to Horse Sweat Saddle and turned his pickup west. His neck ached and his right knee throbbed as he eased the Ford across a rockslide leveled just enough to be officially designated a primitive road.

He drove cautiously over rocks and dips, mulling the difference between petit theft and breaking and entering, between burglary and arson—defined in part by 12 white jurors recalling their beloved town burning to the ground.

By the time he crossed Willow Ridge the road had smoothed to damp dirt. He fought the urge to hurry. His plan allowed for neither chance nor error—no busted tire or punctured gas tank or trail of gear oil from a cracked transmission case. The puzzle's jagged pieces fit neatly together now. His was another flight for freedom, Kamiah and Canada the beginning and the end of the journey. Prudence and history called for an expeditious route.

He checked the pickup's gas gauge at Petersen's Corner and weighed the potential anonymity of filling his tank at Weippe or Pierce. Weippe won. A logging truck entered the road from a nearby clearcut, and Isaac settled invisibly into the truck's dusty wake.

The Ford rolled onto pavement as he approached the single intersection that defined Weippe's city center. On one corner, Durant's General Merchandise advertised groceries, meat and hardware. H & W Mercantile added dry goods to the mill town's offerings. An empty logging truck filled the parking space in front of Swenson's garage. Beside the truck a man worked a tire iron on a split rim wheel, a cigarette pack rolled into the left sleeve of his grease-stained T-shirt. A bright red Pegasus on a swinging metal sign appeared on the opposite side of the street, *Mobil* in blue letters with a red *o*. The sign promised *A Tune-up in Every Tankful*. Isaac pulled his hat low on his head as he turned the steering wheel toward the double gas pumps in front of the station. The forward pump announced gas was 19 cents a gallon.

A station attendant limped out of the storefront, his broken stride the likely result of a widow-maker pine or arm-chaired fir, the sound of a diesel jammer on a frosty morning forever traded for the gas station bell calling the attendant to fill'er up and check the oil. He looked glad to have the work, smiled as he asked the usual, gazed away politely as he pulled the squeegee across the windshield.

"Didja hear about the fire?" he asked as he took three dollar bills Isaac extended through the pickup's open window.

"I've been in the mountains," Isaac told him, a reverse nod of his head over his right shoulder indicating the direction from which he'd come.

"Damned near burned the town down," the attendant volunteered. "Kamiah's Main Street. Sunday morning. Big article in today's *Trib*." The man took the money and shuffled toward the front of the pickup. "Be right back with your change."

Isaac leaned across his pack and rolled down the passenger side window as the attendant rounded the right corner of the front grille. "Any chance I could have your newspaper?" he asked as the man passed by. Isaac wasn't sure what the man mumbled in response. When the attendant emerged again from the station's front door, he carried a folded newspaper in his left hand. He placed a dime in the palm of Isaac's extended hand and laid the newspaper on top. Isaac said "Thanks" from the middle of the cab, then slid back behind the wheel.

The fuel gauge needle swung to full as he pulled away from the pumps. A right turn put Kamiah at his back, Kelly Creek and Montana ahead. A mile north, the smell of freshly milled lumber swept through the pickup's open window as he drove past rows of logs stacked neatly beside a rusted metal roof. A straight stretch of road split dense stands of second-growth fir on either side, narrowing to a distant point. His jaws tensed as he pressed the gas pedal toward the floor. The pickup's front end shimmied at 55, smoothed at 60. On the first curve he could feel the tenuous grip of rubber on asphalt, and his heart began to race.

The wind passing through the open passenger window caught the edge of the newspaper lying on his pack. The newsprint fluttered, then blew open on the seat. William Sheffield stared angrily at him from the *Tribune's* front page.

Isaac slowed the pickup to 60, then 50. Braking sharply, he turned onto a side road to an abandoned log landing. He braked again and came to a stop in swirling dust, turned the key to off and picked up the newspaper.

A third of the page below the masthead was filled with a photo of the pawnbroker standing in a pile of gray ashes and black debris, a rake in hand. The caption read *Business Owner Rakes Through Rubble.* The script below the photo stated *William Sheffield pauses in his search for any objects that might have survived Sunday morning's fire on Kamiah's Main Street. Sheffield is the owner of the former Uncle Bill's Pawnshop.*

Isaac glanced once more at Sheffield's baneful stare. He read the story's headline: *Kamiah Fire Destroys Two Main Street Businesses*. He skimmed the first few sentences, which included reference to the Boots and Saddles Bar. He knew too well the basics. The third paragraph caught his attention. *Fire Chief Bronson Sewell told reporters that the fire likely started somewhere in the pawnshop and quickly spread. Like many older buildings on Main Street, Bronson explained, the fir strip floors were treated with oil, providing a readily combustible surface. He added that a thorough inspection detected no presence of any other accelerant.*

"The fire reached such intensity that it crumbled parts of the brick wall that separated the two businesses," Bronson told the Tribune. "The initial cause of the fire may have been electrical. One of the circuit breakers was tripped early in the process." Bronson also noted that there was no forced entry to either building. "Arson has been ruled out as a possible cause of the blaze."

Isaac read the last sentence in the paragraph again, and then out loud. At the bottom of the article, the paper advised *Story continued on 5A*. He quickly turned to page 5A and began scanning for a lead. Midway down, a smaller headline lurched off the page. *Nez Perce Elder Dies at Stites*. The article was brief. *Friends found the body of Albert Plentyhorses Sunday afternoon in the deceased man's home near Stites. Known to some as Raven Eye, the Nez Perce elder was one of the few remaining survivors of the Nez Perce War of 1877. For many years,*

Plentyhorses lived a quiet life beside the Southfork of the Clearwater River. A Seven Drums burial ceremony will be held Tuesday at sunrise at a location yet to be announced. Further details of Plentyhorses' life will be included in Tuesday's paper.

Isaac lifted the handle of the pickup door, shouldered the door open and stepped to the ground. His knees shook. Dust filled his nostrils as he walked to a stump at the edge of a clearcut that spread south for half a mile. Sorrow and wonder flooded him as he sat beside the road he had followed to this moment. His eyes closed. He held his forehead in his hands, elbows propped against his belly, thumbs pressing his temples. He was still sorting a flurry of emotions when he heard the familiar beat of a raven's wings over the forested side of the road. The bird made no other sound as Isaac watched it fly steadily south along the treetops.

He drove back to Weippe and steered around the rubber hose that would summon the gas station attendant from his battered swivel chair. With a nickel in the pop machine near the station's entrance, a bottle of Coke dropped into place with a clunky thud. Cap pried off, Isaac took a long swallow, then opened the screen door that led to the station's interior. "Thanks again for the newspaper," he said to the attendant now standing beside the cash register that still showed the amount of Isaac's earlier purchase. "Sure thing," the man replied.

Dusk was settling into the draw in front of Isaac's house when he eased the Ford past the last blackberry bush in his drive and stopped in front of his rotting porch. From where he parked, he could see a note pinned to the cabin's door. With one strap of his canvas pack slung loosely over his right shoulder, he moved quickly toward the porch. Scrawled in grease pencil on a piece of grocery sack, the message read *Tuesday morning dawn. We'll gather at the Heart.* Isaac left the note attached to the weathered pine and stepped into the welcoming shadows of his house, dropped his pack on the kitchen table and retrieved a folded piece of buckskin from beneath his bed. The polished handle of an elkhorn quirt appeared as the buckskin unfolded. Reaching into his pack, he retrieved the wadded T-shirt he had placed there when he last parked in Raven Eye's yard. His fingers probed, felt worn canvas threads. He laid the Carlisle artist's ledger book beside the quirt, refolded the buckskin and returned his treasures to their appointed place.

CHAPTER TWENTY-SIX

1953

The sound of boiling water nudged Isaac from the glow of the kerosene lamp atop his kitchen table. Cup of tea in hand, he returned to his mental rehearsal of the coming day. With the first hint of dawn through the single pane window on the south side of his house, he rose, blew out the lamp, and stepped through his front door. The air was still, the draw dark as he walked to his pickup.

Barely visible in the Ford's headlights, the river flowed flat in summer calm, unlike the emotions that coursed through him. Raven Eye's voice filled the cab, scenes and stories chipped and carved into Isaac's mind. An occasional blackberry patch appeared, along with clumps of cattails as he drove east on the route his grandparents had ridden to Sunday sermons, Billy Moses leading, Walking Woman a reticent companion. He passed the flat now covered with wild carrot where his father had watched an auctioneer gavel the sale of Nez Perce regalia to support the war that would end all wars. At the Heart of the Monster, Isaac braked but saw no rigs beside the road, so continued a half mile farther east. Moss covered the shake roof of the missionary house where he had drifted near death on a November night, split cedar fence continuing its merger with the land. The faint outlines of the First Presbyterian Church emerged on his left, white headstones poking into a pocket of fog filling the flat beyond the gravel parking lot.

Headlights approached. A pickup passed, then another, and two cars closely followed. Isaac made the turn, swung around, and reentered the highway. Two more cars and a Chevy van had joined the group at the edge of the field in front of the Heart of the Monster. Figures emerged, their voices low and blended.

"He's with Paul and Jimmy," Luke advised Isaac as the two men came together. "We need two more drummers, then everything's ready." Isaac nodded, thanked Luke for his efforts, felt again the emotional rush that had flooded his morning.

"We did find this," Luke continued, "It was in his lap, his right hand gripped around the shaft. Thought you might want it this morning." Luke extended his arms toward Isaac. The shaft of a pipe tomahawk filled his left hand, his right wrapped around the tomahawk's metal head. Isaac took the hawk and was sliding the shaft beneath his belt when two more pickups pulled up on the side of the road. Window down, the driver of the first vehicle waved his arm down the highway, and Isaac nodded.

They crossed the river in a steady line, headlights on, past the sleeping town as they snaked west on No Kid Lane and pulled onto the flat by the river near the entrance to the cemetery where Isaac's father was buried. The lead pickup had passed beneath the cast-iron arch and parked. Low murmuring rose from the group as they walked uphill through late June grass. A circle of fresh earth near a towering pine drew them forward, the scent of black soil thick amongst them as they gathered. Drummers formed to one side, the rawhide of their drums stretched taut, slender beating sticks held by their sides. The first sunlight of the day highlighted the deep red hues of the Pendleton trade blanket that bound the body of Raven Eye. The drummers began to beat and sing.

On the last of three songs, the throng joined in, high-pitched wails slicing the morning air. A man limped to the front of the group, a broad scar discernible on his right cheek, and stood at the base of the pine where once he had turned in his mother's womb. He sang words familiar as the seasons to this sacred ground, to the river nearby, the hills beyond. *We come from the earth and are cared for by the earth and return to the earth.* Others took up the song, and when the last vibrations from throats and drums had ended, Raven Eye's blanketed body was lowered into the earth. Atop the blanket, the metal head and maple handle of a pipe tomahawk slipped into the grave. Two shovels appeared, and the first dirt hit wool as the full sun cleared the horizon.

Mid-morning, Isaac returned to Kamiah and turned up Main. He glanced briefly at the obvious hole in the familiar scene. The pawnshop's concrete steps led no-where.

One half of the steel vault door hung from its twisted frame, and random heaps of blackened brick poked out from piles of sooty ash. Two men shoveled debris from where the bar once stood onto a flatbed truck, gray dust seeping over the sideboards.

"Some fire, huh?" The grocery clerk grinned as she rang up the sale and advised him nothing exciting awaited him in his post office box. He'd been camping in the mountains, Isaac told her, and had missed all the excitement. She made certain her manager was out of sight before passing Isaac the five extra grocery sacks he requested, then pointed toward the store's nearly empty cardboard box bin.

A half-pound of 8-penny nails was his only purchase at the hardware store, where the missing building across the street elicited no addition to the usual inquiry about whether he needed anything else for his project.

Back in the cab of his pickup, phrases, colors and sounds from the previous year of his life rode with him upriver, down Kooskia's Main Street, across the Southfork Bridge. Awash in scenes, he pulled up to Raven Eye's house and backed his pickup toward the two steps leading to the door.

Inside the house, more scenes appeared: the old man's face, the light of a kitchen candle flickering across wrinkles and the broad scar on the tewat's forehead; thin-skinned hands feeling the nicked edge of the tomahawk head; a greeting smile and the cadence of a song. Isaac took his accustomed place in the rocker, closed his eyes and let the movie run. Raven Eye's voice filled the final scene, the last visit they had shared in this room.

"I had a dream," the old man had said. "Two rivers traveled through deep canyons and dark nights. Each finally took a new path and they flowed together. Many salmon swam up the river, and life was good for the people."

Isaac worked quickly now, retrieving bundles of plants from nails in walls and lowering them carefully into the grocery sacks he had brought from his pickup. Dried roots and berries piled against the west wall were laid gently into cardboard boxes. Isaac hummed as he worked, remembering the time and place of each plant's gathering. Pickup loaded, he decided to capture one last frame, a final page in the chapter of his life that he and Raven Eye had written together. He looked again at the folded blanket on the floor where his uncle often sat. A brain-tanned bag rested beside it, quill decoration confirming it as the one Isaac had brought here just three days before. He tucked the top of the bag beneath his belt and left Raven Eye's house for the last time.

The bell roused Bobby from the lube rack in the Texaco station on Kamiah's Main. He wiped the usual grease from his fingers as he approached what he hoped would be the final customer of the day.

"Oil's good, and I'll do the windshield, just fill 'er up with regular," Isaac directed.

Bobby nodded, popped the gas cap and shoved the nozzle into the waiting hole.

"What's all the stuff in the back of your pickup?" He sensed a story, something he could tell his friends or add to the gossip of the street.

Isaac finished pulling the squeegee across the windshield on the passenger side of his pickup. "Those are my past and my future." He grinned to himself at the cleverness of his remark.

"And what about your present?" Bobby threw back at him, suddenly enjoying this exchange.

"That's why I'm filling up my gas tank." Isaac responded. I'll unload my pickup tonight and leave in the morning. Tomorrow's Wednesday. I have a friend who gets off work at eight, and it's a long drive to Pendleton."